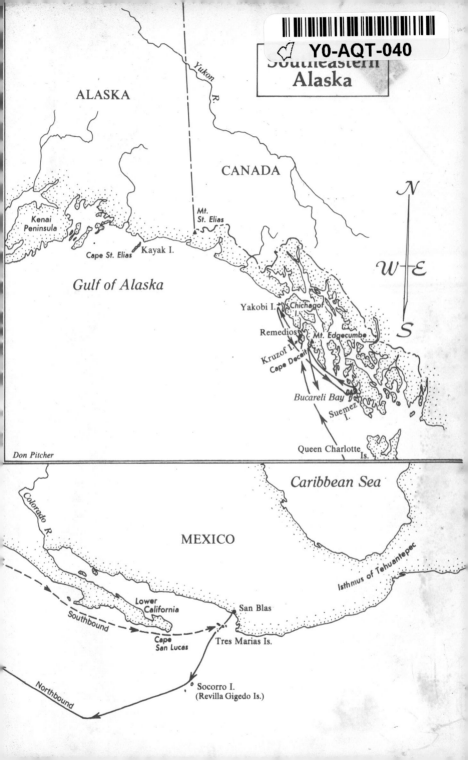

ALASKA

Yukon R.

CANADA

N

Kenai
Peninsula

Mt.
St. Elias

Cape St. Elias   Kayak I.

W   E

Gulf of Alaska

Yakobi I.   Chichagof
I.

Remedios   Mt. Edgecumbe

S

Kruzof I.
Cape Decatt

Bucareli Bay
Suemez
I.

Don Pitcher

Queen Charlotte
Is.

Caribbean Sea

Colorado R.

MEXICO

Isthmus of Tehuantepec

Southbound

Lower
California

San Blas

Cape
San Lucas   Tres Marias Is.

Northbound

Socorro I.
(Revilla Gigedo Is.)

For Glory and the King

For Glory and the King

By

LUCILE McDONALD
and
ZOLA H. ROSS

MEREDITH PRESS / New York

First edition

Library of Congress Catalog Card Number: 69-16297

MANUFACTURED IN THE UNITED STATES OF AMERICA

FOR MEREDITH PRESS

VAN REES PRESS • NEW YORK

Preface

IN 1774 Spain launched her brief golden age of discovery on the Northwest Coast of America. The following year the little schooner *Sonora* made the remarkable voyage herein described, giving King Charles III a claim to southeastern Alaska and strengthening his rights to all of the coast between there and Monterey.

The story is told from the logs of the participants, found in Spanish archives. We have endeavored in our own way to account for the cabin boy, who was one of the three members of the expedition known to have finished the voyage still on his feet.

THE AUTHORS

For Glory and the King

Chapter I

MY father was deserting me! I didn't want to believe it, but it was true. On this very day of March 15, 1775, he intended to leave me here on the beach at San Blas. Never again would I see my home in the foothills.

Father and I had arrived only an hour ago, coming down out of the highlands to unload our donkeys at this tiny port on the west coast of Mexico. Father was in charge of our *patrón*'s donkey train. The animals carried clumsy bales of maguey fiber which the Spaniards needed to make rope for their fleet.

Out in the estuary in front of me were the first ships I had ever seen, and all around me were men rowing boats, carrying casks, spinning cordage, mending sails, and handling buckets of hot tar. The air reeked with the smell of it, mixed with the fumes from the foundry and the stink of the muddy beach when the tide was out.

We stopped at the arsenal to unload the donkeys.

"That's what they need," a villager told us. "Can't get enough fiber to keep up with the ropemaking. Never saw Spaniards in such a hurry."

"What's it all about?" Father asked.

"They're going to explore the far northern part of the Pacific Ocean. They're afraid the Russians are out to grab part of California. No Spaniard has ever gone as far as these ships will. There's never been so much excitement here in San Blas."

I stopped listening to the talk and fussed over the cargo bags on my favorite donkey, Chica.

A man in uniform came out of the arsenal. "That's the port captain," the villager said in a low voice and bowed when the man came over to inspect our supplies. I paid little attention to the conversation until I caught wariness in my father's voice. What was wrong? It was not like him to be afraid.

"I cannot go with the ships," Father declared. "I must return the *patrón*'s donkeys to him."

"Never mind the donkeys. We must have twenty more men," said the officer. He spoke to my father as if he were only another beast in the donkey train, instead of being in charge. Those Spaniards in gilt-trimmed uniforms acted as if they were masters of the world and the sky.

Another man spoke up. "Still, his *patrón* is an important person, Captain."

"Not as important as His Majesty the King." The

port captain turned to my father. "You look able-bodied. You go with the schooner."

They couldn't take Father! How would our family get along without him? My mother worked from daylight to dark, grinding the corn, working in our garden, caring for my little sister and brother. Father glanced at me.

"My son Lazaro, fifteen years old, is strong and agile. If he went in my place, I could still fulfill my obligations to the *patrón*, who trusts me to return."

The port captain and his companion stared at me. I held my head high and stared back, but I thought they looked at me the way the *patrón*'s cook looked at a turkey, judging whether it would be tough or tender. Resentment flooded me.

I was taller than many of my friends at home. My eyes weren't as black as theirs, but the color of brown stones when the sun hit them. In looks I might have been a Spaniard myself, and I hated this. I knew why. Over two hundred years ago, a squadron of soldiers had been assigned to our valley, and one of them had married a great-great-great-grandmother. Not only in my father's family but in my mother's this had happened, and both Spaniards had left their Indian wives and never returned. Spaniards weren't to be trusted. Always I had known this. Never had I been more sure of it than now.

"The boy seems strong enough," the port captain said grudgingly, and though he hadn't put a finger on me, I felt as though he'd poked and prodded me to see if I were sound of limb and wind. "The schooner needs a serving boy. Perhaps this one will do."

I saw the relief in my father's eyes and for a moment I hated him.

"Then may I go, Captain?" Father didn't look at me.

"Yes, yes," the officer said impatiently. "Take your donkeys and get out of our way. Boy, stay here. There'll be plenty for you to do."

The Spaniards strode off. My father and I were alone. Now he watched me anxiously.

"My son, the *patrón* would not have been pleased to see you and not me return with the donkeys."

Chica pushed against me, and I stroked her head. I knew the *patrón* didn't think much of me as a worker. Too many times I'd left the corn when I was supposed to be in the fields. I took my beatings without whimpering, and the *patrón* didn't like that, either. He would have been easier on me if I'd wept and promised to do better. Somehow I couldn't in front of that man who might order me and my family to do anything. Only the *señora*, the *patrón*'s wife, kept me out of more trouble.

When she brought me to the big house to do her errands, I tried to please her. When she taught me to read and write, I worked hard. She praised me and suggested to her husband that I'd be helpful in the estate office.

The *patrón* grunted, but finally said he might give me a chance when I was a year older. I liked the idea. Now this could never happen.

"Lazaro." My father put his hand on my shoulder. I looked at him and saw the shine of unshed tears in his eyes. He did care, I knew. For a moment we were silent in shared sadness, then my father's fingers pressed hard.

"Lazaro, do not rebel. It will only make things harder. Oh, my son . . ."

Chica butted me in the ribs, and I clenched my shaking hand in her rough coat. I can't stay here, I thought wildly, even as I obeyed my father's command to roll my sandals in my poncho. Into the bundle also went my extra shirt and the small fife I could play better than anyone in our village.

"I won't be able to play at the next feast day," I said.

Father put his arms around me. He held me as he had not done since I was a small boy. Then he released me and wordlessly started the donkeys toward the hills. He did not look back, but Chica did, braying at me, as if to ask why I wasn't beside her.

A swarthy, big-shouldered Spaniard called, "Here, boy!"

I went because I had no choice. The big man looked me over as the port captain had done. "I'm the boatswain. My name's Santana. What's yours?"

"Lazaro Sanchez."

"Come with me. See those wooden rollers on the beach? It will soon be high tide and we'll have to shove the schooner into the water. You can help push."

He shouted for more men and we followed. Beside the schooner, he handed me a long, stout pole.

"Brace it against the hull, boy. Now all together."

The sticky mud squished between my bare toes. I

slipped but managed to keep my balance. The schooner was newly caulked and pitched on her bottom and would be ready to sail with the rest of the fleet. Cables and something called capstans helped us get her into the water. When it was done, my muscles were sore and my back ached.

That night I slept on the hard ground in the shadow of the arsenal. I closed my eyes and pictured Father trudging toward the hills. Was Chica missing me? Did my father long for me as I did for him? What would my mother say when I didn't return?

Here I was in the world of water, of jungle, of ships and sailors and Spaniards. I had been stolen from my world of rolling hills and corn and maguey and donkeys and fiestas. Weary from my work, I slept, but I kept waking through the night, my hatred of the seacoast and the Spaniards flaring higher and higher.

In the morning Pedro, a friendly sailor, showed me where to get some *frijoles* on a *tortilla*, and then Santana was at me again. "Do this!" "Carry that!" I helped roll casks of salted meat to the *lanchas*. My shoulders strained under bales of ham and cheese, sacks of beans and corn and lentils.

Because I could not help it, I learned strange words signifying the different parts of the ships. There was my prison, the schooner on which I was to sail, and I soon discovered that it was the poorest of the three vessels in the estuary.

I eyed the other two ships. The largest, the *Santiago*, was called a frigate, and the packet boat was the *San*

Carlos. The frigate, I heard Santana say, was ninety-one feet in length. That seemed long to me, but Lieutenant Ayala, master of the schooner, sneered at its small size. He was even more scornful of his own vessel, no more than thirty-nine feet long.

"This *Sonora!* Only thirty tons and can't carry most of her own provisions," he declared. "If we get separated from the frigate, we'll starve."

I didn't like the sound of that. Pilot Mourelle, the second officer on the schooner, was contemptuous of San Blas as well as the ships.

"What a navy!" he exclaimed. "San Blas isn't my idea of a naval base. Nothing but a landing place in the midst of mangrove swamps. Look at that mucky beach!"

Most of what the officers said was a mystery to me. Why would they sail on ships they despised? They weren't trapped as I was.

I watched the small boats go back and forth with supplies for the voyage, and when Santana was busy in the warehouse, I slipped away. I'd learned how to vanish when I worked in the fields of the *patrón*.

There was no one at the back of the long building, and I leaned against the wall, staring glumly about me. How I wanted to go home! I bent and picked up some pebbles at my feet.

I threw high, aiming at the floating debris in the water. I would hit nothing; the distance was too far. That didn't matter. For this brief moment, I was I— Lazaro Sanchez from the hills—not a mosquito-bitten, two-legged donkey to be ordered about by the Spaniards.

One second I was alone, the pebbles flying through the air. Then a man was in front of me. I had drawn back my arm for another throw, and it was impossible to halt the motion. The pebble flew. It struck the man's tricorn hat. It bounced from his head and rolled in the mud. I just stood there. I couldn't lower my arm or make my feet move.

In my terror, I was sharply aware of the Spaniard, of his uniform of fancy blue broadcloth, his red waistcoat and gold buttons. His shoes had gleaming buckles. He reminded me of our gaudy Mexican birds when they strut. He wasn't much taller than I, but when he scooped up his dirty hat and advanced upon me, he looked like a giant. Would he shout for other Spaniards? Would he have me bound and whipped until the blood came? Even in the hills we had heard tales of the Spaniards and their cruelties.

"Who are you, boy?" He did not shout, but his eyes were hard.

"Lazaro Sanchez," I stammered.

"And what are you doing, skulking behind the warehouse, throwing stones at officers of the King?"

There was no answer to that. I was silent.

"Well, Lazaro Sanchez, who are you? What are you?"

"I—I am to be serving boy on the *Sonora*," I muttered.

"So?" He brushed at his muddy hat, looked with distaste at his fingers. "Then why are you not on the beach working to get her ready?"

Why didn't he get on with it? Why didn't he shout for someone to punish me or do it himself?

He continued to look at me. "You are one of those recruited yesterday, I think. And I'd wager a stranger to the sea?"

I would answer. If I was to be beaten, what difference did it make what I said now? Father had often told me my tongue was my enemy. Let it be that way.

"I come from the hills. And I wish I were back there!"

That would earn me an extra whiplash, but I didn't care. I hated this Spaniard. I wished his hat had been knocked out into the water and that a wave had swept it away forever.

A strange expression crossed the man's face. "Who goes where he wishes?"

Anger surged through me. Let him beat me to death! For the last time I would speak my own thoughts.

"A Spaniard can do anything he wants to do! He can come into our country, take us from our homes, and imprison us aboard his ships! And we who were born here can do nothing at all!"

I stepped back, expecting a blow, but his eyes glazed over and it was as if he didn't see me at all. Then, without another word, he turned and walked rapidly away.

What would happen now? Oh, Father was right. My tongue was my enemy. This Spaniard would surely whip me. I had to see what he was going to do. I followed him, keeping distance between us, though he never looked back.

Briefly he was out of sight, but when I sidled around the far end of the large adobe building, he was talking to two men. One was Lieutenant Ayala, master of the schooner; the other was the port captain.

I sneaked behind a stack of baled caulking fiber, careful to keep out of sight. Suddenly I wondered what ship the man with the tricorn hat commanded. It wasn't the *Sonora*, and I was glad. What were the three men saying about me? I strained to hear. Why, they weren't talking about me at all! They were speaking of the schooner. The stranger, I discovered, was Lieutenant Juan Bodega y Quadra, a friend of Lieutenant Ayala. He wanted to sail on the *Sonora*. My fear was replaced with anger. He had forgotten all about me. I wasn't even important enough to be beaten.

I longed to hear what they said. At last, I caught a word.

"Don Juan, this must be decided by Don Bruno Heceta," the port captain said.

"Then let's talk to him," Lieutenant Bodega demanded.

The three men headed toward the commander of the fleet, some distance away, and I felt more confused than ever. Lieutenant Bodega looked determined and excited, as if bent on making an important point. Whatever he said was close to his heart. My curiosity mounted.

They talked and talked. Finally Don Bruno smiled and threw up his hands. When he spoke, I knew it was exactly what Lieutenant Bodega wanted to hear, for he looked as if he might toss his hat in the air and whoop, as I did when I won a race. Lieutenant Ayala laughed so hard that many turned to stare.

What had happened? I burned to find out and spoke to Pedro about it. Pedro grinned at my questions and, as I'd expected, knew what had happened.

"Don Juan," Pedro explained, "was supposed to stay in Tepic, miles inland, but when he came to San Blas, pretending he wanted only to say good-bye to his friend Ayala, he talked Don Bruno into letting him sail on the schooner, even though he must take orders from Ayala, who is the same rank. Bound to go with us, Don Juan was. He'll stop at nothing."

I couldn't speak. This Spaniard who would stop at nothing was the man whose hat I'd knocked off, the one I'd shouted at behind the warehouse. What would happen to me now?

Chapter II

ALL day Santana kept me hard at work. I didn't try to get out of it, for I reasoned that Lieutenant Bodega might not remember me if I was in the midst of other seamen. I caught a glimpse of him from time to time, but he paid no attention to me.

"All right, boy," Santana said, when I'd carried the last of many clay jars of lard to be rowed out to the ships. "See that you get your bundle and are at the landing place when the sun's at the western horizon."

I scurried off before he could think of more work and stretched out in a shady spot near a palm tree that overhung the sea wall.

Besides the lard, we had carried crates of live chickens to the frigate. Beef cattle were already mooing in pens on the *Santiago*'s deck. I felt sorry for them. I was as

penned as they were, though I didn't suppose the Spaniards intended to slaughter me as they did the cattle.
Food that would spoil went aboard the vessels last. The
Sonora carried no animals, for she was too small. I'd
heard the only reason she was going along was to explore shallow harbors where the frigate could not enter.

I drifted off to sleep, wondering what would happen
when Lieutenant Bodega noticed me again. When I
wakened, the waterfront was empty and quiet. The ships
were still out in the estuary, but where were the men?

A child came by, herding a pig, and stopped to stare
at me.

"Aren't you going to sea with the ships?" he asked.

"Yes." I sat up.

"Then why aren't you at mass with the others? They
are all at the church on the hill. Don't you want to be
blessed and return safely from the voyage?"

I jumped to my feet. Why hadn't I heard about the
mass? Perhaps if I ran, I could still receive a blessing.
No, it was too late. The men were coming down from
the hill. Santana saw me and beckoned.

I brought my bundle and sat where he pointed in the
lancha, on the bottom boards. My stomach felt hollow,
and I wondered if I was seasick. A seaman who had
made one other voyage had told me that seasickness was
like a plague. To keep my mind from my stomach, I
listened to the talk of the officers. I was still surprised
that they thought the *Santiago* and the *San Carlos* small.
In Spain there must be ships larger than any I could

imagine. How far away was Spain? I'd thought the journey from home to San Blas long.

Lieutenant Ayala kept grumbling about the schooner.

"If we're to map the entire North Pacific coast of America," he declared, "we ought to have seaworthy vessels."

"We'll manage," Lieutenant Bodega said. "This is the kind of assignment I've wanted all my life."

"On an elegant craft like this?" Lieutenant Ayala jeered.

"On any craft. This is the most important expedition Spain has ever organized on this coast." Lieutenant Bodega's expression was serious. "Rather than wait until another expedition is sent out—and who knows when that will be?—I'd sail in a longboat."

"All right, all right, forget what I've said." Lieutenant Ayala laughed.

We drew alongside the schooner and the officers leaped from the bobbing *lancha*. The deck was so low that I scrambled aboard without trouble.

"Take these to the cabin, boy." Lieutenant Ayala shoved something like a blanket at me. Lieutenant Bodega added another to the heap and I saw they were blue greatcoats. I had never seen anyone wear such heavy garments in our hot climate.

There was only one cabin, reached by the companionway toward the stern. Seven steps down and I was in the hold, pushing my way through the door to the right of the stairs. In the tiny cabin there was no place to hang the coats. You couldn't stand up straight in the cubbyhole except just inside the door, where it was over the keel. I threw my burden on the lower of two bunks. This wasn't much of a place for a ship's master. Its only furniture was a chest, over which there was a shelf which could be pulled down from where it was hooked against the wall, making a small table.

I backed out of the cabin and looked around. Provisions were stacked so solidly in the hold one could barely squeeze past them. Where could I put my own bundle? I couldn't sleep in one of the eight narrow bunks built into the walls up forward, for there were twenty of us besides the officers, and I was the least important member of the crew. Not only Santana but everyone aboard had made that clear.

Someone else felt the same way. "Where am I going to sleep? Hang myself over the side of the ship?" It was a sailor called Miguel Rodriguez. He wasn't much older than I, and I'd seen him being cuffed several times. His hair was red; it made him stand out, for it shone like polished metal, with shades of a sunset.

Santana glared at Miguel. "The deck won't be any harder than the floor of the jail," he said and jerked his head at me. "Find yourself a place on the coils of rope, boy," he advised.

"A nest in the spare canvas is better," Pedro told me. As he went by, stooping under the weight of his sea chest, he pointed to a spot where several layers of sails were lying over the water casks. I crawled there and saw I could make a burrow for myself, so I tucked my bundle into the niche before anyone else claimed it.

I was none too soon. Miguel was making for the same spot when I turned. Our eyes met.

"How did they get you on this tub?" he growled.

I told him. He was the first one who really listened. The others didn't care.

Miguel grunted. "I'd have run off. Me, I'd no choice. Those cursed Spaniards hauled me out of jail."

"Why were you in jail?"

He shrugged. "The keeper of the *cantina* forgot to lock the door. I drank a bottle of his *aguardiente* and borrowed a few coins from his box. He caught me."

I stared at him. I'd never known a thief.

"Miguel!" Santana roared.

"I'm coming." Miguel tossed his last words at me from the corner of his mouth. "But I'll get off this tub, you'll see. The Spaniards can't keep their eyes on me forever."

Was there a way to get off the ship? Miguel thought so. Could I take the word of a fellow from jail? Why hadn't I tried to escape? When the men were at mass, I might have run toward the hills. If I'd overtaken Father, he wouldn't have turned me back. The Spaniards might have sent someone after me, though. Too late now. If there'd been a way out, I'd slept through it.

I watched the other members of the crew stow their belongings in the hold. It would have been nice to lie in a corner where I could raise my head without bumping it. No matter. Santana said I could sleep on deck as long as the weather was warm.

The hold measured only eight feet at its deepest, but

now the hatch in the center was wide open. Canvas was stretched above it to keep out the rain.

After sunset, we had only the dim glow of the cook's lantern. The hold was a shadowy mass of barrels and bales, with ropes and gear dangling around us and the butts of the masts rising up through the middle. The brick firebox, with its iron smoke vent poked through a hole in the deck, was the principal object forward. The berths, in tiers of two, hugged close on either curving side of the hull, and pots hung from hooks fitted to the timbers.

I was to take orders from Carlos, the cook, but he said nothing to me, so I watched the sailors, noticing one who placed his blanket on top of the rice sacks. His name was Tomás. He, Miguel, and I were the youngest of the crew. From his complaints about the tight space and Pedro's answers, I learned that Tomás was a fisherman. He had been on a lighter delivering casks of drinking water to the ships.

"You shouldn't have bragged about how strong you were," Pedro jeered. "That's why the Spaniards grabbed you."

Tomás muttered. I gathered that he, like myself, had had no choice. I felt better that two others on board were as unhappy as I. From what Tomás said, I guessed that he, like Miguel, was determined to escape. How? The officers, the quartermaster, or the boatswain would seize anyone foolish enough to make a try.

"When do we sail?" I asked Pedro.

"They'll fire a cannon," he told me.

I kept expecting to hear it, but it was ten o'clock before a gun boomed on the *Santiago*. The *Sonora*'s anchor was picked up and the sails let out. The hollow feeling returned to my stomach. This was it. Now I was a sailor who couldn't go back to land until the voyage was over. I watched the frigate and the packet boat pass us. Their white canvas shone in the moonlight. Had the *Sonora* moved? What was I expected to feel? Then I heard Pedro beside me. "Holy Mary, are we going to stand still all night?"

I waited and waited and was almost glad when Carlos told me to carry mugs of hot chocolate to the officers on deck. They were in the stern and not as lively as when they'd come aboard.

"The lanterns at the arsenal are at about the same distance as when we lifted anchor," Lieutenant Ayala muttered.

"At first I thought strong currents held us back," the pilot said. "But that isn't so."

"Maybe the *Sonora* is just contrary," Lieutenant Bodega suggested.

I lay on deck, as Santana told me to do, and all night I kept waking, wondering what was going on. The officers tried every trick with the canvas, but nothing worked.

In the hour before dawn I stirred. What had disturbed me? The ship was still. I heard snores from the hold, the faint lapping of water against the vessel. I raised myself on my elbows and almost yelped with surprise.

Miguel, on all fours, crept past me toward the bow. As I watched, he saw me and put a finger to his mouth. He let himself down over the side, clinging to the gunwale. Now he was in the water, almost without a sound. He was going to swim to shore! Oh, if I could swim! I'd have been over the side after him. Envy of Miguel stabbed me.

But we'd reckoned without Santana. He shouted at Miguel, then with a loud splash was in the water, swimming strongly, overhauling Miguel immediately. The crew was awake, watching. Now we saw one head, now two. Santana's fingers closed in Miguel's bright hair. His fist came up and connected with Miguel's chin. He turned back, towing his captive. When the two were pulled on board, Miguel was still unconscious.

"Good work," called Lieutenant Ayala. "Keep an eye on him when he comes to, bo'sun." He wheeled on us. "Any of the rest of you thinking of leaving?"

What would happen to Miguel now? Lashing? Bread and water? Would he be shoved into the tiny rope locker up forward? Pedro had pointed it out to me. In there a man could barely move.

Miguel sputtered awake, and Santana hauled him to his feet.

"Another trick like that and it's the locker for you, boy!" he threatened.

Miguel swore and rubbed his chin, but he didn't answer, nor did he make any more trouble that morning.

When full dawn came, the day was hot and airless. There was no wind at all.

Miguel was still subdued when he claimed his bowl of porridge. Only Pedro spoke to him.

"Make up your mind to stay aboard, boy?" he mocked.

I heard Miguel mumble "Never," too low for Pedro to hear. I was surprised. Did Miguel still imagine he could escape?

Far in the distance the frigate and the packet boat were waiting for us outside the harbor at the white rock that had been colored by the many birds that roosted there. The *Sonora* still sat in the estuary.

"Even if we could walk on the water and push," Lieutenant Ayala fumed, "we wouldn't budge this snail until an offshore wind springs up."

I didn't know what to do with myself, but I'm always good at napping, so I found space on deck and curled up, pulling a fold of canvas over me for shade. It was hot on the schooner, but it was hotter on land. I fell asleep wishing for the cool, pleasant highlands.

Carlos wakened me with the toe of his shoe in my ribs. Others were stirring from sleep when I went below to carry the evening meal to the officers. Cook ladled out bowls of stew from a large, tin-coated copper pot, and I took food to Pilot Mourelle on deck and to the two officers in the tiny cabin. Lieutenant Ayala sat on the locker to eat and Lieutenant Bodega bent double, crouched half in and half out of the lower bunk. Their faces were cheerless.

"Don't you wish you'd stayed in Tepic and waited

for another ship, one with space for eating your meals?" taunted Lieutenant Ayala.

"Any ship is better than none. *Amigo,* to be a part of an expedition that will add to Spain's greatness . . ."

"I know, I know!" Lieutenant Ayala smiled at his companion. "With you aboard, we won't forget the importance of this voyage. Right now, may God give us a decent breeze."

As if in answer, we heard a rustle of movement on deck and a ripple against the hull. The lieutenants rushed out to find Pilot Mourelle already ordering sails spread to catch the wind off the land. This time we moved, sedately, like an old lady. Green leaves floating on the water sailed along faster than the *Sonora* with the breeze puffing out her mainsail.

"Her cargo must be stowed wrong," Don Juan said. "We'd better shift it."

"Let well enough alone," Lieutenant Ayala retorted. "She's moving, isn't she?"

At sunset we were outside the estuary, with the white rock much nearer. Then the wind dropped. I'd never before known a dying wind could be so important. Don Bruno must have seen we wouldn't make it to the rendezvous and sailed to meet us.

"Where did you learn to navigate?" he shouted from the frigate's quarterdeck, speaking horn in hand. "You're holding all of us back."

"The cargo must be stowed wrong," Lieutenant Ayala replied. "We'll shift it." Under his breath, he mut-

tered that Don Bruno wouldn't do any better with this
schooner.

"Now that we're away from land, she'll move along,"
Don Juan predicted.

"I hope so!"

We were far enough from shore so that I saw the hill
country rising behind the mangrove swamps. My father
would be somewhere on the upward trail. I wished I
were, too. Men didn't cry! My father had always told
me that. While I did not cry, I felt a swelling in my
throat as if I had swallowed a chili pepper whole.

We anchored for the night and set out at dawn with
another land wind. Though we made a good start, we
soon lagged far behind the other ships. Lieutenant Ayala
and Pilot Mourelle fussed around, ordering this and
that done with the sails. Don Juan went into the hold
to study the positions of meat kegs, water barrels, spare
anchors, all the heaviest objects. He came over to where
I was seated on the plank deck scouring porridge from
the cooking pot with a handful of maguey fiber.

I'd heard Lieutenant Ayala say that all Mexicans
looked alike to him. I hoped Lieutenant Bodega was
that way, too. My fingers were thumbs as I waited for
him to mention his ruined hat, but before he spoke,
Lieutenant Ayala called to him.

"Juan, I've figured how to set the topsails to catch
the land breeze by night and the sea breeze by day."

"Good!" Lieutenant Bodega hurried to deck. "If we
anchor the minute the wind drops, we'll not lose ground
because of strong currents."

Now we were far enough offshore to feel the sea's movement. My stomach was uneasy, and Pedro teased me.

"Seasick, boy? You'll get used to it."

I doubted it. I felt worse all the time. I was pulling up a wooden pail of seawater in which to wash bowls, mugs, and spoons. I almost dropped it when a cannon boomed. The *Santiago* and *San Carlos*, anchored ahead, were waiting again.

Lieutenant Ayala groaned. "Here comes another lecture!"

"Not this time," Pilot Mourelle said, "there's a distress signal on the *San Carlos*."

A red pennant fluttered from the topmast. Distress? What did that mean? When we reached the other ships, every man was on deck. Before we could launch our dinghy, the *Santiago*'s longboat was pulling across to the *San Carlos*.

Miguel nudged me. "Look at that officer waving his arms. What's he up to?"

I glanced away from the frantic officer aboard the packet boat and looked at the white rock astern. We were only two days out of port. Would we turn back? I prayed that we would as I watched the officer of the *San Carlos* go first to the frigate, then head for us.

Why, that man in the longboat was Don Diego Manrique, the packet boat's captain. He rolled his eyes, and was brandishing a pistol. I didn't wonder his seamen looked ready to duck, but our officers greeted him politely and agreed that they'd accompany him to the frigate.

"They're holding a council," Pedro muttered. "What for? Looks to me as if Don Diego's gone *loco*."

"If he has," Miguel hazarded, "we might all go back to San Blas."

"Even if we do," I argued, "won't they just put us to work on another ship?"

Miguel sneered. "Not me, boy. Once on shore, all the Spaniards in San Blas won't find me in the swamps."

"Nor me," Tomás murmured.

Could I slip away to the hills? I could try, I decided, and jumped when Carlos shouted for me.

All night we lay at anchor, Pilot Mourelle in charge, all of us tense, waiting for news. By daylight men made bets about how soon we'd head back to San Blas.

Our officers returned at noon, Lieutenant Ayala grinning, Lieutenant Bodega very serious. What had happened? As they climbed aboard, Lieutenant Ayala greeted the pilot.

"Francisco, meet your new captain, Don Juan Bodega y Quadra, by orders of Don Bruno himself. *I* am commander of the *San Carlos*."

"What? Is Don Diego dead?"

"No, but completely addled in the head. The surgeons bled him, but it did no good. Back he goes to San Blas."

"Poor man," Lieutenant Bodega said, "to come with high hopes all the way from Spain and now—"

"Too bad, but that's it." Lieutenant Ayala turned to

me. "Lazaro, gather my gear and put the chest into the skiff."

I obeyed, fighting disappointment. Only Don Diego was going back. The rest of us must sail north.

When the boat was ready, Lieutenant Ayala embraced our new captain.

"Into your hands go the fortunes of the *Sonora*, Juan. You said any ship was better than none. Still think so?"

"Go with God, my friend," Lieutenant Bodega answered.

As I went about my work, I wondered if he knew that the crew was unhappy over our change of command.

"Fancy buckles won't navigate this snail," Santana grumbled.

The crew neither knew nor trusted Lieutenant Bodega. Lieutenant Ayala had been a great man to laugh, had even laughed at Lieutenant Bodega himself, who was smaller than the other officers, quieter, more elegantly clothed. Pedro said what I was thinking.

"Forget turning back," Pedro declared. "That Bodega sailed when he was supposed to stay behind. He'll go on, no matter what happens."

Nobody answered him, but men began to talk about the bad omens with which this voyage had begun. How could you depend on a ship that took two days to get out of the estuary?

"It's unlucky to change officers, too," Antonio, the quartermaster, put in. He told a story about a vessel that went down in a storm. "Right after a shift in command!"

"Cease your croaking, man," Santana rebuked. "*Two* ships have changed officers. Maybe the *San Carlos* will draw the bad luck."

When we ate, I took my bowl and sat near Tomás and Miguel.

"I saw you carrying wine to the officers," Miguel said. "Precious little wine we get."

"If I'd been at the oars of that longboat taking Don Diego to San Blas," Tomás complained, "I wouldn't be on this schooner now."

"Just wait till this cursed tub touches land," Miguel said.

In late afternoon we dropped anchor, and I heard the officers talking about their maps.

"If we go as far north as the King orders," Pilot Mourelle said, "do you realize we'll be near the Arctic Circle and past every Russian discovery? If we meet the Russians on the way, what then?"

"Commander Heceta will decide that. This voyage is in search of information. If, through us, the King learns the truth about what the Russians are doing, he can deal with the court in St. Petersburg. I tell you, Francisco, if we take possession of land on the way, we'll be modern *conquistadores*."

"You're a dreamer, my friend."

"Always," Lieutenant Bodega admitted. "All my life I've waited for something like this. My family was against my going to sea. One brother became a professor. Another a lawyer. I'll show them, I vowed, but I was nineteen before I entered the Naval Guard. I'm thirty-one now. Ofter I thought I'd go mad as I waited."

"And then you were sent to North America," Pilot Mourelle said.

"Yes!" Don Juan's eyes glowed. "I'd always longed to explore this West Coast. And then I was almost left behind!"

"Juan," the pilot declared, "a man who makes his own luck as you do could never be left behind!"

I told Pedro about this conversation and asked him about *conquistadores*.

"To the Spaniards a *conquistador* is a hero," Pedro said. "One who takes possession of more land for his king."

As I curled up for the night, I thought about Don Juan determined to be a hero. He'd take the rest of us to the Arctic Circle. Where was that? What was it? That it was a long way, I was sure. It had a cold, forbidding sound. I didn't want to go there. I thought of home. I wanted to smell the scent of chili ground on a stone *metate;* I wanted to eat the ears of sweet corn, fresh from Mother's field.

Miguel and Tomás felt sure we could escape. I'd go along with them. Anything was better than the chance that we might die, deep in the unknown, driven by Don Juan's dream.

Chapter III

NEXT day the breeze was medium fresh, and we got under way again as soon as the longboat returned to the *San Carlos*.

"I'll wager Don Diego's all right now he's back in San Blas," Miguel said. "If I thought I'd get sent back, I'd act crazy myself."

"You wouldn't have to do much acting," Tomás jeered.

Miguel ignored him. "No use," he decided. "Only officers get favors when they're crazy. Us, we'd be shoved into rope lockers."

I thought he was right.

Lieutenant Bodega set about transferring the weight of the cargo toward the prow and the stern. Carlos was cross, for he still needed space up forward. Pedro grinned at me when I stumbled over a netful of hams that had been knocked from its overhead hook.

"Your nest in the canvas is gone, boy. I'm no better off. Our bunks are barricaded with casks."

I was too busy to worry about my sleeping place. Once Lieutenant Bodega helped me push a heavy barrel. I was so surprised I was more awkward than ever. As if he sensed my astonishment, he grinned at me. With his red waistcoat and frock coat removed, he didn't look much different from the rest of us. He was clearly disappointed hours later when he and Pilot Mourelle agreed that cargo shifting hadn't improved matters.

"The other ships are leagues ahead and gaining all the time," Pilot Mourelle complained.

"They've furled everything but their topsails and still we can't keep up. Never mind, I'll try another idea." Lieutenant Bodega wouldn't admit the schooner was just plain contrary.

Whatever he tried, it didn't work. There was a great hauling and knotting of ropes as the sailors spread the foresail at a crazy angle.

"Waste of time," Pedro told me. "We'll strain the mast."

Lieutenant Bodega must have reached the same conclusion. He mopped his face and turned to the pilot.

"I see Don Bruno has anchored. We'll get more advice through the horn."

We didn't, though. Don Bruno must have formed a poor opinion of the foresail antics, for he signaled that he was putting a towline aboard us. The schooner mustn't slow down the entire expedition.

Our officers exchanged hopeless glances. A dinghy came from the frigate, letting out a heavy cable as it approached. Santana had men ready to take the line and attach it to the windlass up forward.

"A fine command," Lieutentant Bodega mourned. "To be dragged along at the end of a rope."

It worked. We began to move.

Now the ocean had opened into a wide nothingness except for several little islands. Behind us the mountain ranges on the mainland loomed dimly. There was not a canoe or a fishing boat or another ship to be seen.

After we took the towline, our mariners had little to do but stand their watches and sleep. They talked about their villages and of the ports where they had worked. Only five had been to sea, in fishing boats or carrying freight along the coast. Pedro was the most experienced traveler, for he had been on the *Santiago* during the Perez voyage. Santana had been on trips to the missions.

When the men ran out of other subjects, they gossiped about the expedition, and I learned that Commander Heceta and the other officers from Spain had nearly missed making any voyage at all. They had been so long arriving in Mexico that the viceroy became impatient. He sent Pilot Perez north the previous summer. Perez was now on the *Santiago,* under Don Bruno.

The frigate didn't return until after Commander Heceta's party reached Mexico City. Nobody was happy with the Perez voyage. Santana spoke scornfully of Perez.

"He saw new country, but he didn't have the courage to go ashore, plant a cross, and claim the land for Spain. So now Commander Heceta is supposed to do it, and in case the harbors are too shallow for the frigate, we're along to explore for him in the schooner."

"Why should we risk our necks when Perez wouldn't?" Miguel demanded.

Pedro laughed. "Only officers can choose, lad. Not us. Perez went as far as he thought safe."

I thought of Lieutenant Bodega, who could have stayed in Tepic. Pilot Mourelle said a man made his own luck. Officers, maybe, not crews. We took orders. The pilot was only four years older than I, but he was an officer and understood almost as much about ships and charts as our captain.

The morning after we got the towline, Pilot Mourelle told me to bring him the spy glass; a red-legged gull was flying around and he wanted to look at it more closely. When I came back from the cabin and was almost beside Don Francisco, the schooner heeled suddenly. I lost my balance, dropped the brass tube and came down on top of it. I might have slid overboard with the spy-glass, but the pilot grabbed my shirt, reached under me and rescued the instrument. Then he pulled me to my feet.

"I'm sorry, sir," I stammered. "I couldn't help it."

"Fool!" he snapped.

"I've never been on the water before," I said. "I'm not from San Blas. I'm from the hills."

"And in a week, you haven't learned to stand up or be trusted with ship's property. Boy, I sailed before the mast when I was twelve, under masters who tolerated no nonsense."

He turned his back on me and I scurried below, where I found Pedro hanging up neatly coiled lengths of rope. I told my story.

"He'd have let me go overboard if the spyglass hadn't been under me!" I sputtered.

"Why not? A spyglass is more important than a cabin boy." Pedro laughed. "Mourelle's a hard man. He's a poor relation of Spanish nobility and takes himself seriously. He wanted to attend the Royal Academy, but his parents couldn't afford it. He learned navigation in the pilot corps school."

"What's that?"

"Starting at the bottom. All Spaniards aren't rich, boy, though compared to us, they are. Take Don Juan Bodega, who comes from Peru."

"Peru! Aren't all Spaniards from Spain?"

"Ho! Don't they teach you anything in the hills, boy? Spain has colonies and Peru's one of them. Don Juan's father was sent to Peru to hold a government office. He married there. His uncle is rich and important. That's why Don Juan is called Bodega y Quadra. His father took the uncle's name because he believed it would improve the family's fortunes. But Don Juan didn't want to do anything but go to sea, and finally he enrolled as cavalier in the Naval Guard and next thing was ensign on a warship."

The things Pedro knew astonished me. Santana was wise, too. From them, I learned that Don Bruno was commander of the officers sent from Spain because he was the oldest. Pilot Perez was outclassed by them, since he, like Mourelle, hadn't attended a naval academy.

When I passed on what I'd learned to Miguel and Tomás, they only hooted.

"Listen to Lazaro, the Spanish sailor!" Tomás mocked. "Who cares about the officers? I want to get off this schooner!"

"Lazaro's mad because he's less valuable than a spyglass," Miguel taunted. "Give up, boy. Don Juan would heave any of us over the side if he thought he'd get more speed that way."

I believed that. Only the *Sonora* and her movements were important to our officers. I wished I could leave this ship and never see her again.

What jobs I drew! I fetched salted beef from the casks, ground corn in the stone mortar, ground hot peppers in another mortar, scoured pots and mugs and bowls. I cleaned up anything that was spilled. I kept the officers' cabin in order and if I didn't have those blankets in the berths the way the Royal Armada ruled, I had to do it again, the pilot standing over me, his cold blue eyes missing nothing. I was tired of poking and crawling into small spaces, taking out and putting away the supplies Carlos wanted. I felt stooped and wanted to stretch and run. I'd have hoed the *patrón*'s entire corn patch just for the joy of having that much space in which to move.

Even my fife was no comfort. Twice I took it out and played, but once Carlos yelled that I sounded as bad as a cat yowling, and the other time Pilot Mourelle ordered me to remake the berths in the cabin.

On a day late in March, when we were near the Tres Marías Islands, the *San Carlos* hoisted a signal. There was hand-waving and hallooing, and Pedro said the packet boat was leaving us to deliver supplies to the mission and fort at Monterey in Upper California.

"Then Lieutenant Ayala will sail farther north and explore San Francisco Bay," Santana agreed. "They're founding another mission there. But the frigate and schooner will continue to sail straight west."

"Why don't we go north, too?" I asked.

"What an empty head you have, boy," Santana rebuked. "The coast of North America is not a straight line. It extends northwest, and we must go west to meet winds to carry us north. Haven't you learned that much about sails when you've seen the lieutenant try every combination these past weeks? We must get out where the winds blow that will carry us in the right direction. Then maybe we'll navigate without a towline."

The Marías Islands dropped out of sight behind us. The wind blew fresher, the ship rolled, and I had to learn to keep my balance. Pots in the galley swung and banged against the timbers; nets of onions and peppers swayed overhead, and one day the swells were so rough there was no cooking at all. We munched bread and cheese. All that night the ship rocked, the spray splashed high against the schooner, and the men fastened planks over the open hatch. From then on the hold was reached only by dim rays of sunlight, and a brawny man like Santana had to stoop to avoid bumping his head unless he was in the center of the vessel. I'd thought it crowded before; now we were shut into a dark little box, tossed back and forth without ceasing.

As I washed the officers' linen in a bucket of seawater and fetched their meals, I listened to their talk. They agreed that the *Sonora* was a poor excuse for a ship, though Don Juan said its small size was necessary to carry out its purpose. Both men grumbled about the mistakes on the new maps brought from Spain especially to guide the expedition.

At noon each clear day one officer held up an instrument called a quadrant and looked at the sun and the horizon, measuring an angle which told them how far north we had sailed.

"Look at that!" Lieutenant Bodega exclaimed in disgust. "The maps show the Marías Islands farther north than we know them to be.

Pilot Mourelle looked at the other small island in sight.

"There's the last land we'll see west of San Blas," he commented.

How did they know this was the last land we'd see to the west? I sneaked a look at the maps. Could I make anything out of these papers they thought so important?

I bent over the wall table. The chart looked like

witchcraft to me; I struggled to find meaning in the lines. Suddenly a hard hand came down on my shoulder and spun me around.

It was Lieutenant Bodega, his brown eyes stern.

"The boy who throws rocks at officers!" It was the first time he'd mentioned it. "What are you up to now?"

"N-nothing, sir."

"Don't lie. Have you touched these papers?"

"No-no, sir, only l-looked at them."

"I seem to remember you didn't actually touch my hat, but it was the worse for your being around."

"Y-yes, sir. I—I intended to apologize."

"Sometimes apologies are worthless. That would be so if anything happened to those papers because of your carelessness."

He slapped the table for emphasis. "Never put your fingers on those maps unless they are in danger. Water must not drip on them. They must not blow away. They're valuable now. They'll be more so as we go along and the pilot and I mark shore lines and place names. Do you understand?"

Before I could answer, Pilot Mourelle's harsh voice cut in. Because of his fairness and his blue eyes, he always reminded me of snow and ice in the hills.

"I'd say that boy is more dangerous than water or wind! He nearly lost the spyglass a few days ago."

"He will not lose the maps," Lieutenant Bodega said. "Go now. Henceforth, mind what you do."

I scuttled away and later told Tomás about the papers. Miguel drifted closer to listen.

"I wish the wind would blow the maps overboard," Tomás declared. "Then we might head for land."

"You suppose those maps are worth money?" Miguel asked. Even in the cramped space where we huddled, Miguel was relaxed and grinning.

Tomás and I exchanged glances. We knew that Miguel managed to tap the wine barrels and once had stolen *aguardiente.*

"You been at the wine again, Miguel?" Tomás demanded.

"Why not?"

"You'll get yourself beaten," I warned.

"Or into the rope locker," Tomás added.

"Oh, I'm luckier than that," Miguel said.

I looked at him with admiration. I always felt better when I was with Miguel and Tomás. They talked of escape, and, when I listened to them, I believed it was possible too.

"Keep your ears open, Lazaro," Tomás told me. "You might hear something that will help us once we get on shore. Got any raisins?"

I reached into my pocket and shared the sweets. The other two teased me because when I could I pilfered raisins or bits of cheese, onions, or peppers. When Carlos caught me, he cuffed me, but that didn't stop my doing the same thing again.

"Sneak some dried meat and wine when you have a chance," Miguel said. "When a fellow's on the run, he doesn't want to go hungry."

"Carlos keeps too close a watch on meat and wine," I said. "Besides, where could I hide them?"

Listening to the officers, as I was told, I heard a lot. Lieutenant Bodega's odd watch fascinated me. It was as big as the palm of his hand, and Santana said it showed how far we were from the capital of Spain. I heard more about maps, too. Our best one was made by a Frenchman from information supplied by travelers of all nations.

"Does Upper California go as far as the ice?" I asked Santana.

"What do you know about ice, boy?" He was stretched on his bunk and grinned at me.

"Snow is in our Mexican mountains. On Don Juan's map where lines are dim, this Frenchman wrote 'Unknown.' The lieutenant says only travelers, fur hunters, and Russians have seen the ice. What about the Russians?"

"Who knows? If this expedition maps and explores the coastlines, then the Russians can't steal part of California."

"Weren't two Russian ships the first to sight the coast?" Pedro asked. "They put out from that cold territory on the ocean's western shore, didn't they?"

"Who knows?" Santana said again. "Maybe they weren't there at all. The ships were separated and each captain saw something different."

"They were there," I said.

"Well, well, listen to who's making a big noise."

Santana sat up. "How does our big brain from the hills know that?"

"It's on Don Juan's map." That was what "Land viewed by Chirikov" and "Coast discovered by Commander Bering" had meant. "The writing said 'sea west of Canada,' " I added. "What's that?"

"Another part of North America where only fur traders and hunters go," Pedro replied.

For days there was hardly any wind. Our officers, working on the maps, grew impatient. To Lieutenant Bodega the towline was a disgrace. I couldn't see why. What difference, as long as we sailed?

We talked back and forth to the frigate, using signals or sending messages in a small corked barrel that was pulled along the towline. The eighty-fathom cable was handy for hitching a cord to it and letting out and drawing in the barrel.

One day Miguel told me excitedly that Don Bruno planned to send men ashore at Socorro, the last island that they knew about.

"He wants water to refill his barrels, forage for the stock, and wood for a new foretopmast. They've mended theirs twice now with lashed rope. I wonder if anyone from the schooner will be sent ashore?"

I wondered if they intended to try for escape there, but Tomás put an end to this thought.

"Look at the place." We were ten miles off.

It was brown and barren, with steep bluffs and currents so strong we couldn't get close. Miguel sighed.

"No use to make a break there. A man'd starve to death."

I looked forward to stepping ashore anyhow. Two weeks we'd been on this chip of wood, twelve feet wide, thirty-nine feet long from stern rail to prow tip. Twenty-two of us, sick of our cramped quarters and each other.

"I feel like a chicken in a crate," I complained to Santana. He laughed and called me Little Rooster.

The wind died and we were swept along by the currents, farther and farther from Socorro. We'd let go the towline the night before. Don Bruno signaled frantically that we must tack, use the schooner's oars and not get separated from him.

Everyone took his turn at the oars. After two hours of pulling on these great blades, I felt as if I'd been beaten. We were too weary to grumble.

That day Carlos made a stew with dried peppers, onions, *garbanzos* (chick-peas), and a piece of fresh veal that had been killed on the frigate and sent to us.

"Carlos isn't a bad cook." Tomás scraped the last bit from his bowl.

"Ahh!" Miguel wrinkled his nose. "Everything tastes alike. Stewed weevils, mildew, and scrapings from dirty kettles."

"Maybe you'd like wine or *aguardiente* poured over your meal," Pedro suggested.

Tomás and I exchanged glances. So Pedro knew what Miguel was doing. Hardly a day that he didn't tap a wine barrel. I worried that he'd be caught and whipped.

Next morning Don Bruno issued new orders. The

ships couldn't get near the island without more wind, so he'd put out his longboat and tow the schooner closer. We must use the oars and try to cross the strong currents holding us offshore.

For three days we rowed. By the second day I was numb to the sting of blistered palms, for the aches in my swollen wrists and arms were torture. I would have sworn my back was broken in two, but still, with the others, I bent to the oars.

Don Juan sent the pilot to ask how much longer this must go on. He reported that Don Bruno agreed we'd leave in the first favorable wind. While the calm lasted, we must keep on trying.

We rowed until late on Sunday, the second of April, the longest day I'd ever endured. Resentful grumbles rose from the crew. Why should we work so hard when the frigate officers did nothing but order us to row some more! When I went to sleep at sundown, I was so sore I might have been beaten. A few hours later I was jarred awake with a crash. There was a terrible scraping sound as I scrambled from my nest.

We're sinking, I thought. I rushed on deck and saw that the tide had caused the *Sonora* to drift against the side of the *Santiago*. Cursing men tried to push us away with poles, but our anchor had snagged in the frigate's mainsail and the canvas was badly torn.

There was no light but that of the stars and a few dim lanterns. The ships rasped against each other with woeful skreaks. There was a confusion of arms, legs, ropes, and oars. I should have stayed below, but I was too terrified. If we broke open a seam, the water would pour in.

That little deck was no place to be when twenty men were struggling to keep us from crashing. Most of the crew was on the starboard side; their weight tilted the narrow deck. They pried and pushed with their hands.

Santana saw me. "Hey, Little Rooster! Over here!"

I got to my knees, braced against the gunwale, hands out to push. In a breath I was flying down into the black water between the ships.

The salty seas closed over me. The ripples were rimmed with phosphorescent light. I choked. I couldn't swim. I would die.

Chapter IV

THE currents sucked me into the blackness. Then something fastened on my shoulder. I was yanked from the water and dragged over the side of the longboat. My cheek scraped against an oarlock.

Shouts aroused me. I opened my eyes. There was enough light to see the shadowy figure of Santana snubbing a line to a cleat on the schooner. Pedro reached for my feet and together the two men hoisted me aboard and laid me belly-down over an empty cask at the foot of the companionway. Pedro rolled me back and forth. My arms and legs flapped; I gagged and salty water spewed from my mouth.

Carlos brought a mug of hot broth, but I couldn't swallow.

"Don't waste soup on him," Tomás laughed. "He's already gulped half the southern sea."

The carpenter uncorked a gourd full of *pulque*. "This will fix him, make his feet bigger so they can stick to the deck." He dribbled the fermented maguey juice between my lips.

I jerked away. "Leave me alone!" I touched my sore face. My cheek was raw. Tomorrow I'd have a black eye. I could hardly see out of it now.

Pedro thumped me on the back. "Easy, Little Rooster. If Santana hadn't been quick, you'd be food for the fish now."

"Then I'd be off this crazy boat!" I yelled.

What had happened came back to me. The ships must be free of each other now, for the *Sonora* no longer grated against the frigate.

Lieutenant Bodega pushed through the men. "Get out of those wet clothes," he ordered. "I don't want a sick sailor aboard."

Miguel brought my poncho and a scrap of blanket. I stepped out of my water-logged shirt and pants. After a while, I stopped shivering and crawled into my roost. I kept seeing that awful blackness closing over my head.

The other men went back to work or to sleep, but Miguel stayed beside me, talking in a hoarse whisper.

"Didn't do much good for yourself, did you?" he said. "Me, I want to be alive when I get off this schooner."

"I'm not so sure I care, just so I get off!"

"Oh, yes, you do." In spite of his mockery, the tone of his voice told me that he was my friend. He put his hand on my shoulder before he left me. He was kind.

Often he gave Tomás and me a helping hand. Though he jeered at our thanks, he was there when we needed him.

The next day I had to stand a lot of teasing.

"Never knew you wanted off this tub that bad!"

"He was on his knees when he went overboard. Were you praying, Lazaro?"

"Always a waste of time, praying," Miguel declared.

For a week I put up with this. The jokes stopped only because there were too many other things to plague us. The weather grew cold. We plowed through a gray mist and Don Juan, ever cautious, placed pails to catch the moisture dripping from the canvas. In a pinch, we would have extra drinking water. The *Sonora* plunged and pounded at the end of the cable, and slate-colored swells broke over the bow in clouds of spray. The deck was always awash, and we worked in clothes that were wringing wet.

Don Juan hadn't wanted a sick sailor. He had two now, lying in their bunks too ill to move. Other seamen had to find new places to sleep. We'd eaten our way through part of the rice, onions, and dried peas. I still helped myself to bits of onions and peppers. Chewing them between meals took away the monotonous tastes of weevily porridge, beans, and stew.

A brisk southeaster carried us along in the right direction and Don Juan welcomed it, crowding on every possible inch of canvas.

The *Sonora* had taller masts than most schooners, and far above us the square topforesail filled with wind and the rigging hummed in the blast. We plunged and hauled; often we heeled so far over that the sick were pitched from their bunks. They lay and groaned. Carlos and I helped them back up, but there was nothing anyone could do for them.

Lieutenant Bodega fretted about this. "Francisco," he said, "as soon as we can handle the skiff safely, I'm going to the frigate and insist on medical care for our sick."

I hoped he'd get it. I was sorry for those sailors. Their mouths were sore; their joints ached. They couldn't sit up to eat and they shivered all the time. Their blankets were always damp, and the rolling and the tossing of the schooner gave them no peace. They slid about on the hard bunks, bumping against the sides.

"Why don't they yell and swear?" Miguel demanded. "*I* would."

"Too sick to make the efforts," I told him. "If I ever get like that, I'll wish I'd drowned when I fell overboard. Carlos says they have scurvy, the sickness many men get at sea."

"Who knows?" Pedro said. "Most of these fellows have never been off dry land before; everything looks bad to them. Santana's calling us, Lazaro. I'll bet we'll row the lieutenant to the frigate. He's bound to get some medicine."

I took an oar, as Santana ordered, and we rowed easily to the *Santiago*, for the wind had lessened. We waited in the skiff while Lieutenant Bodega and Commander Heceta were in the officers' quarters. Frigate sailors talked to Santana and Pedro through the portholes.

"You picked the wrong ship, Bo'sun," one man said. "I hear you're being sent back to San Blas. Don Bruno's tired of coddling you like an unweaned baby. Too bad. The *Santiago* will win all the *saludos* from the King."

"Don't laugh too soon," Santana cautioned. "You may be shipmates with us yet. You might change bunks with our seamen who are too sick to work."

"Blessed Mother, let's hope not!" The man fell silent when the officers appeared. The surgeon, who was with them, refused to allow any of the schooner's crew aboard.

"Our men are down with fever. Yours would only catch it and be worse off," he stated.

Don Juan turned to the commander. "Then give me seamen to replace those who can't work."

"Impossible. Still, if any man wishes to volunteer, I won't object."

I watched our captain and saw signs of anger in his face. I hoped he would argue with Don Bruno, who might become so furious he'd send schooner and crew back to San Blas.

"I don't think any volunteers will appear, Lieutenant," Don Bruno said.

I looked eagerly at Don Juan. After a bit, he bowed, descended the ladder into the skiff and said not one word as we rowed back to the *Sonora*.

Plenty was said later when we talked among ourselves. Why couldn't we give up and go home? It seemed forever since we'd been on this ship.

Next morning the drizzle stopped. For the next three days the seas were calmer, though waves still sloshed across the deck. We carried full sail when there was the least breeze and I couldn't remember when I'd been warm or dry.

One dreary day followed another. The ship creaked and rolled; the waves slap-slapped the sides; we stayed at the end of the towline.

"The farther we go, the farther we'll have to go back," Pedro said. "Why not turn around before worse happens?"

Others agreed, but Santana smiled and shook his head.

"We won't turn back while Don Juan's at the helm. He says all will be well when we reach the River of Martin Aguilar."

According to Don Juan, the sick would recover on land, fresh water could be supplied; a new foretopmast could be found for the frigate.

"River of magic," Miguel scoffed. "Me, I don't believe there *is* such a river."

Later I heard Santana ask Don Juan about it as the two men stood at the poop rail looking out across the water.

"Sir," said Santana, "except for Pedro, no one ever heard of this river before. Even Perez never saw it."

"So you wonder why I'm so sure it's there, Bo'sun?"

"Yes, sir."

"A Spanish captain saw it as far back as sixteen hundred three. That year two ships sailed from Mexico, commanded by Sebastián Vizcaíno and Martin Aguilar. They reached north latitude forty-three degrees."

Santana had told me latitudes were locations officers learned from their quadrant.

"These two captains," Don Juan continued, "discovered a cape, which they called Blanco. Sickness aboard forced the ships to turn back. Aguilar, sailing farthest, sighted a great river on the north side of Blanco."

"And lived to tell about it?" Santana asked.

"No, but his sailors reported his discovery when they rejoined Captain Vizcaíno and a priest wrote down what they said."

"And though no one has seen this river since, you believe it is still there, sir?" Santana spoke doubtfully.

"Come, Bo'sun, rivers don't run dry."

"No, sir."

Santana wasn't satisfied, I was sure; neither was I. I'd heard of mirages, when things seemed to be real but weren't. Suppose this river was a mirage? Why couldn't Don Juan turn back?

All day my anger grew. If Don Juan wasn't stubborn, we'd be headed home. The wind was more favorable, and both officers looked satisfied when they went below to sleep.

I could hear them talking as I rolled unhappily in my damp clothes.

"Juan," Pilot Mourelle asked, "when is a dream impossible?" Before Don Juan could answer, he went on. "Do you think we ever really had a chance on this expedition?"

Don Francisco wanted to turn back too. I sat up,

eager to hear Don Juan agree, but his first words told me he wouldn't.

"A dream's never impossible, Francisco, if men of good will put forth every effort. Come, isn't one Spaniard worth three Russians? If the Russians reached the unknown, why can't we?"

I couldn't hear the pilot's reply, but I gathered what was meant. Lieutenant Bodega believed that Spain's future in North America was at stake on this expedition. Unless it succeeded, Spain might lose what she had already won and never extend her empire farther on this coast. Oh, I understood how Don Juan felt, but I didn't care about kings or empires. What were my chances of staying alive in the unknown territory ahead? I didn't think they were very good.

Early the next morning I went on deck. The breeze had freshened into a brisk blow and I noticed that Antonio had taken a reef in the *Sonora*'s mainsail. Just before Don Juan turned in last night he'd ordered the watch to keep on full canvas while we had a following wind.

"Who told you to do that?" I asked, pointing aloft.

Antonio frowned. "Stick to your pots, boy! The frigate's reefed. I'll not be the one to overturn us."

If I'd come within reach, he'd have clouted me, but I was wary. I'd had too many cuffs from him. I eyed him sourly. I was sick of him, of this ship, of everybody aboard. If I told Don Juan what he'd done, Antonio might get worse than he'd given me. I'd get even. I was down the companionway and into the officers' cabin in seconds. I put my hand on Don Juan's shoulder and his eyes flew open.

"Yes, boy? What is it?"

"The quartermaster has reefed the mainsail."

Now that it was too late, I wished I hadn't told. Don Juan leaped from the bunk. He couldn't have grown taller, but he looked it. I hurried after him as he rushed to deck, brushing Antonio from the helm.

"Shake out that canvas!" he ordered and seized the tiller.

Antonio jumped for the lines. In fear or in haste, he tripped, sprawling at the lieutenant's feet. Then he was up and others helped him tug at the halyards, until the sails were as Don Juan had set them.

Other sailors jammed the companionway, Santana among them.

"Bo'sun!" Don Juan shouted. "Summon the crew! I want every man to hear this!"

"Yes, Captain."

Men straggled to deck, to the foot of the companionway. We were so close I could hear the harsh breathing of those beside and behind me.

"Who reefed that sail?" Don Juan demanded.

"S-sir," Antonio stammered, "the frigate took in her sails. I didn't want to risk—"

"*You* didn't want to risk! The pilot or I decide on the risk! From this moment no man lowers one span of sail unless we say so. What the *Santiago* does is not our business. Shall we let them believe the *Sonora* is manned by cowards?"

His breeches were rumpled, his feet bare, his shirttail flapping. No matter. He was our commander. Even Miguel had respect in his eyes.

"You've heard talk that we're turning back. It's a lie! You've worked in wet clothes. So have I. Some of your fellows are sick. So are men aboard the frigate. Until now I believed we had one thing lacking aboard the *Santiago*—staunch spirit."

He paused. No one spoke, but I fumed. He could talk! He was in command.

His tone changed. "We'll improve our condition," he promised. "You'll see when we touch land. When we succeed, as we will, we'll share the glory." He glanced at Antonio. "Quartermaster, I didn't dream that authority would be stolen while I slept."

Antonio wriggled and did not answer.

"We must trust each other," Don Juan went on. "In this endeavor, we must act as one."

"I meant no harm," Antonio murmured.

Miguel's whisper tickled my ear. "A wizard, that Don Juan. With his spell on us, we'll be drowned before we know it."

"Come," Lieutenant Bodega said, "are you with me?"

Several grinned sheepishly; a few nodded.

"Santana?" Don Juan questioned.

"I'm with you, sir."

"You, Carlos? You, Pedro?"

"Yes, yes."

Don Juan's glance took in the rest of us, settled on Miguel and Tomás.

"You two. Will you sail my course or try out your own?"

"Yours, sir." Miguel wasn't as brash as usual; his fingers scraped nervously through his bright hair. Tomás mumbled agreement.

"Good, that's what I like to hear. Carlos, some wine to warm us. Let us drink to our partnership."

"Good, that's what I like to hear," Miguel mimicked. Only Tomás and I heard him.

Carlos handed me a great basketry-covered jug. I carried it so that everyone in the crew had a drink. I did, too, but I was still rebellious. What real choice had we? Don Juan might call us partners, but he gave the orders.

Later I talked with Tomás and Miguel.

"Oh, you're right," Miguel agreed, "and if the pilot were in top command, we'd get orders without so many fine words, too. Or without wine." He licked his lips. "Oh well, why worry? If we get to that river, we'll go ashore. Don Juan may want glory. Me, I want off the schooner."

Escape! I mulled it over all week. It would be dangerous, but I didn't care. Anything would be better than sailing on and on.

Don Juan might think he'd stiffened our backbones, but I knew better. We did what we were told, but we complained among ourselves.

The weather dealt us mists and sudden squalls that shifted swiftly from one quarter to another. Then we had spells of dead calm. Still we bobbed at cable's end.

Still there was no sign of land. No sign of the River of Martin Aguilar, either. The men muttered that Don Juan had made fools of us with that story.

The twenty-first of May dawned cold and rainy. I woke up shivering and miserable, the eternal swish and splatter of water on the deck a few inches above my head, the creaking and straining of the ship repeated in my aching bones. It was too rough for a fire in the galley. We'd eat cold gruel or go hungry. I fished in my pocket and found a fragment of hot pepper. It tasted as flat and moldy as everything else.

We were grumbling over our gruel when the watch reported that the frigate was signaling. The little keg was pulled along the towline with a message from Don Bruno. From it we learned that he was calling another council meeting.

"How can we launch a boat in this sea?" Santana demanded when the officers went to their cabin.

I wondered too. The northeast wind had kicked up a wild sea, but I knew Don Juan would go to the *Santiago* if possible. We speculated on the reason for the meeting. Could it have to do with a decision whether to continue on our course or to turn back?

"Pilot Perez and others on the frigate have had enough," Santana told us. "Not every officer is so set on glory as Don Juan."

The morning advanced. The sails were furled. The waves menaced. Don Juan called the crew together but could hardly be heard above wind and waves.

"We can't attend the council meeting!" he announced.

"But we'll send our opinions in writing. I want you to hear Don Bruno's message. I'm going to read it to you."

This was *it*—our chance to turn back, I was sure. The commander's note was demanding.

"We must decide what to do to make our limited water supply hold out. The seamen are weary and we must act. Tell me your opinion. Shall we go to Monterey or continue on our present course?"

Tomás nudged me, and Don Juan raised his voice.

"The pilot and I are against return. What about our crew? Do you feel as you did on the day we had trouble with the sails? Or do you wish to go to Monterey?"

We had our chance to speak out. Why didn't Santana or Pedro or Antonio say something? Why didn't I? But I was the youngest member of the crew. If I opened my mouth, Carlos would thump me with his cooking spoon.

The silence held, and Don Juan's smile flashed.

"Good! I'll read you my reply." He held the paper firmly against the tug of the wind. "On no pretext do Pilot Mourelle and I wish to go to Monterey. We can bear our hardships until we reach the River of Aguilar. If we lose time by going to Monterey, we could not carry out the King's orders this year."

His tone emphasized each important word as he continued. "It is late to change plans. My men are with me in the desire to take a chance on acomplishing what we have been sent to do. God will strengthen and aid great actions and if we should reach such bad straits that we can find no remedy, we are willing to die, each at his own task, for the glory of the King."

Don Juan looked at us expectantly, and then Santana raised the cry. "For the glory of the King."

The cheer went up, raggedly at first, then strongly. I myself cheered and was surprised to hear Miguel's voice, too. Don Juan had a way about him.

Color came into his swarthy cheeks. He smiled proudly at us, rolled the messages together, and placed them in the keg. He pushed the cork into place. Antonio started the container on its way across the slate-gray water.

I watched the keg move along the cable. We had to go on! Miguel and Tomás had planned on escape in Monterey.

"There it will be simple. We can go inland," Miguel had said. "There are valleys like paradise, I've heard men say."

"And streams where we can fish," Tomás had said. We'd heard a lot about that fishing boat on which Tomás had worked. It had belonged to his father, his uncle, his three older brothers. When he was old enough, he would have his own share.

"You and your fish!" Miguel had said. "But yes, in the valleys are many streams. And game I can snare or shoot with arrows. Oh, there are so many ways to live on the land."

The keg with its fateful message had reached its destination. We watched a sailor remove the paper and give it to Don Bruno.

"Never mind," Miguel spoke up. "Maybe Don Juan's right. Maybe we will find the River of Aguilar. What difference where we hit land? Escape may be even easier in a place other than Monterey."

Tomás brightened. "Why not? I'm sure you're right, *amigo.*"

Things weren't so bad when I had friends like Miguel and Tomás. "When we get off this tub..." we said to each other. The words comforted me by day and by night. I no longer thought, "If we escape..." Now I said, "When..."

Chapter V

FOR the next week we were in choppy seas. The *Sonora* rolled so much that we staggered about like drunk men.

"But we don't have that happy reason of too much wine," Miguel lamented. "Oh, when I'm off this ship, I'll never come within a league of anything that floats. If only I'd stayed out of that *cantina*."

Don Juan tried to hearten us by saying we were sailing landward, but I often doubted it. Land seemed as far away as Heaven.

On the sixth day after Don Bruno had accepted our decision to go on, we were becalmed. Gray clouds enveloped us; we were in a world without light or life, and we were always cold. That morning Miguel refused to eat.

"Shall I bring some gruel?" I asked.

"I don't want anything."

"Cheese?" I'd sneak it somehow.

"No." He swallowed hard.

"Are you sick, Miguel?"

"Sick of this ghost ship! Leave me be!"

Fog encircled us so that we could no longer see the frigate. Later in the day Tomás came to me.

"Miguel gave his stew to Pedro, who's always hungry. Miguel hasn't been at the wine barrels again, has he?"

"I haven't seen him. And I've been working within plain sight of the casks."

"Still, he can slip around mighty sly. He'll get beaten yet."

I tried to keep an eye on him, but he avoided me and when I washed the officers' linen, I lost sight of him. Again Tomás came to me.

"Miguel's asleep. He goes on watch at midnight. Did he eat tonight?"

"I don't know. I was busy."

"He says the stink from the hold turns his stomach. Mine, too, but I eat."

"Let's go to sleep and forget it."

Easier said than done, for the sour, moldy stench was everywhere. When I'd peeled onions that day, I found their centers so rotten that Carlos threw them out. If only we'd reach land! I wanted to find a place where the sun shone and Tomás, Miguel, and I could escape so that never again would we see, touch, or smell the *Sonora*.

I woke from deep sleep to hear sharp voices. I jerked upright. What new disaster was upon us?

"We'll take him to the surgeons on the frigate, Santana," Don Juan said.

"Will bleeding cure a man of drunkenness?" Pilot Mourelle demanded. "The boy reeks of *aguardiente* as well as wine. We should have checked those casks more closely. No wonder the bo'sun couldn't rouse him."

Miguel! If he couldn't stand watch, he was in trouble! What were they going to do with him? I rolled from the blanket and crept up on deck.

The fog still surrounded us. The lantern made eerie shadows, streaking the faces of our officers and Santana as they stood over someone who must have been carried to the deck. Miguel! I was sure of it!

"At daylight we'll take him to the frigate," Don Juan said. "I'm not sure it's only drink . . ."

Miguel ill, not drunk? Back in my nest, I couldn't sleep and was in the galley the next morning before Carlos. When Tomás came and I told him my story, he slapped his forehead.

"I knew he'd get in trouble!"

Santana called me. I was to help him and Pedro row Miguel to the frigate. I tried to get a good look at him, and as we started our journey I touched his hand. His skin was as hot as charcoal.

"Pedro! Is Miguel dying?"

Pedro snorted. "Getting drunk never killed anybody."

"Wonder if they'll take him aboard the frigate?" Santana said.

Don Bruno didn't object, however, and Miguel was lifted aboard and carried to the doctors. Pedro and I waited in the dinghy until Santana returned.

"Will he be all right?" I asked.

Santana shrugged. "Miguel's swigged enough spirits to save him from the devil and all the angels."

I tried to take comfort from this, but I couldn't. At supper Tomás and I talked.

"Maybe he'll think it's worth a beating to have all he wanted to drink for once," Tomás said.

I couldn't believe it. That night I was lonely. Silly, I told myself. How could anyone be lonely on a ship that was so crowded? Yet the hollow emptiness in me persisted. Next morning I hurried on deck to stare across at the frigate. If Miguel was to be beaten, surely he'd be sent back to the schooner for his punishment.

Later, Don Juan went to the frigate, but I wasn't sent along to row. In the next hour Carlos scolded and cuffed me, for I couldn't keep my mind on my work. When the dinghy returned, would Miguel be in it? He wasn't, and when Don Juan went to his cabin, I spoke to Pedro.

"Miguel isn't dead, is he?"

"Of course not. But the surgeon says he has a fever and drink made it worse. He can't stand, and he won't be coming back here."

"Won't be coming back! Why?"

"Don Bruno thinks such a wine thief is safer where he can be locked in a brig."

Tomás and I looked at each other in despair. No Miguel! How could we bear it?

"Oh, well." Tomás tried to be cheerful. "If we're close to land, as Don Juan says, we'll see Miguel ashore. Maybe he's lucky. The frigate's a lot bigger than the schooner, and I'll bet the food's better, too."

"I wish he could come back, just the same," I said.

I was still gloomy the next morning, and the day matched my feelings, gray and cold. I was on deck when Don Juan exclaimed so loudly that I turned in alarm. He was laughing.

"Land ahead, boy! And when we're on shore, half our troubles will be over!"

"Land, sir?" How could he say that when there was only water in sight?

"Look at the signs!" He pointed to long tails of brownish-green kelp carried by the currents. Floats the size and shape of oranges were attached to the streamers.

"What are they?" I asked.

"I don't know. Let's call them orange-heads."

Excitement spread. Next day we saw a bright-green plant, like extra-long blades of grass. Ducks, fish, and seals bobbed and flashed in the water.

"But where's the land?" Tomás demanded.

"Don Juan says it's very near!"

The officers talked about the findings of the quadrant and the French map.

"If Perez was here," Pilot Mourelle said, "why didn't he map along the way?"

Santana set up his own cry. "The towline's broken!"
"Spread all sails!" Don Juan shouted.

It took time to catch up with the frigate; it took longer to mend the broken cable. Impatiently, I watched for land. Would we ever see it?

Then suddenly, on the seventh of June, we did see land. I hung over the rail. How soon would we touch shore? How good to feel earth under my bare toes, to drink sweet water! Again bad luck brushed us, for the winds died and we were becalmed.

A night and another day. Then the winds favored us, the towline was hauled in, and Don Bruno signaled us to follow his prow.

"That coast looks rugged," Don Juan worried. "It won't be easy to find a suitable port."

I couldn't stop looking. Those green mountains! There would be meadows and gullies and little beaches. Small streams, too. My mouth puckered. The water ashore wouldn't be this brackish stuff we'd had for so long.

"Harbor beyond the point!" Pedro cried.

There it was, a landlocked cove! Tomás crowded close to me.

"What'll you bet Miguel's planned our escape down to the last thing?" he murmured.

Tomás hadn't forgotten. Neither would Miguel. I longed to listen to their schemes.

The schooner moved ahead of the frigate, Antonio heaving the lead line up forward. In such places the *Sonora* was important. We moved into the bay, Don

Juan happily planning repairs as soon as we were anchored.

"Three months and twelve days from San Blas, Juan," Pilot Mourelle said. "A long voyage."

Long! It had been forever! As soon as I was free of this prison, I wanted to forget every minute.

"*Ai!*" Santana's voice scaled upward. He pointed and we all looked.

From the north side of the harbor, Indian canoes were heading for the *Santiago*.

Indians! I wheeled on Tomás. In his face, I read my own dismay. Miguel hadn't taken Indians into account!

Chapter VI

NEVER had I seen Indians like the ones who approached fearlessly in four dugout canoes. They were naked except for seed necklaces and twists of grass, feathers, and flowers in their hair. They stood up, gesturing and smiling. Their bodies were painted and they had wrapped strings of hide or feathers about their legs.

They weren't shy, though they approached cautiously. We saw bows and arrows in their canoes, as well as short wooden clubs studded with sharp pieces of flint. They were as determined to meet us as we were to land on the shore. I wished the *Sonora* were larger as the four canoes came too close to us. Why, the Indians were smiling! When Santana offered them beads, spoons, and gewgaws from a trade-goods chest, the savages were more than friendly.

"Look how pleased they are with those few bits of glass," Tomás whispered. "Are those otter and deer skins they have in their canoes for exchange? Maybe those Indians will come in handy for us. They might show us trails, help us to escape."

"But we don't speak their language," I said.

"Santana's getting along all right with making signs and stuff," said Tomás.

All the time the savages hovered, the pilot kept a seaman flinging the lead line and sounding for an anchorage. He steered for a cove between the cape and a huge pinnacle rock that stood out from shore. He signaled the frigate to approach, that he had found a safe harbor. We saw springs of water dripping from the high bank above the sandy beach. A small stream emptied into the bay south of the big rock.

I had hoped I'd be chosen to go with the first party sent ashore for water. Don Juan told Santana to take a boat crew to fill the barrels. As we rowed across to the brook, I looked eagerly toward the frigate, at anchor about twenty fathoms astern of us. Miguel might be with the party from the *Santiago,* and it would be easy to spot his bright hair.

I forgot about him when I stepped on land. I was bewitched! I couldn't walk! I lurched from side to side, my legs going this way and that, until Santana roared and caught my elbow.

"Steady on, boy. Not seasick on land, are you?"

"My legs are!"

Others joined in Santana's laughter, and the Indians

watched curiously from a distance. I hated being a show for them too, but in minutes I got my bearings and the ground no longer rocked beneath me. I plowed through sand to the edge of the stream, dropped on my knees and sank my face into the water.

When I'd drunk my fill, I looked around me. Land! How wonderful! What giant trees! Santana said they must be strange pines; I neither knew nor cared. Away from the darkness of the forest were tangles of wild roses, their scent sweet on the air.

A second boat came ashore. Tomás rushed past me and fell on his knees as I had done.

"The barrels," Santana ordered. "When we get those filled, and the firewood party has its work done, we're free for the rest of the day."

What a shout went up! How we worked! Never were tasks finished so swiftly. Santana grinned when he gave us the word.

"Stay together," he warned. "The Indians seem all right, but I don't trust the heathen."

Pedro picked shellfish from the rocks and tossed them into a caldron. Carlos was doing the same thing. Both stuffed some into their mouths as they worked.

"What are they, Carlos?" Tomás edged close and I followed.

"Mussels. Try one. They're like the oysters on the beach at San Blas."

Tomás and I pried open shells, eating twice as many mollusks as we dropped into the kettle. Suddenly Miguel raced up to us. He too ate his fill.

When our hunger was eased, the three of us went off together to find a stream and bathe. As naked as the savages, we washed ourselves and our clothes in the clear water, spread our garments to dry, and lay on the warm earth. No one paid any attention to us. We were as alone as if the others were in San Blas.

"Ah-h!" Miguel let out his breath with contentment. "Land! Trees! Fresh water! Oh, I swear to you, I've sailed my last mile with the Spaniards."

"Three months," Tomás said. "Three long months."

"It wouldn't take us that long to get back to Mexico!" Miguel's eyes were eager. "All the world knows that across the mountains there is a gentle slope leading to Mexico. Once we're away from the sea, we'll live on game I'll shoot and fish Tomás will catch." He sent a roguish smile toward me. "Game and fish Lazaro will cook."

Tomás frowned. "We need a net or hooks to catch fish and a musket with which to shoot game. Unless you can use a bow and arrow like the savages?"

"Why not?" I put in. "I can make and use bows and arrows."

"Good," said Miguel. "Plenty of muskets and pistols aboard the frigate. If you don't believe I can steal one, you don't know me."

"It should be possible," Tomás said. "I'll get twine for a net, maybe even a hook or two. What about the Indians?"

Miguel laughed. "What about them? You've seen

them, anxious to please, giving skins and food. Why, they'll help us as we go along."

"But all savages may not be so friendly," Tomás objected.

He was the practical one, and I looked at him with respect. Miguel was full of tales of gold in the valleys. Once we reached them, he claimed, we'd find the precious metal that Coronado had sought so long ago.

"I'll be satisfied if we get home," Tomás declared. "Gold I've never seen much of, but given fish to catch, valleys with water and game—that's enough for me."

"Me too," I echoed. I longed for home, for the clear air of the highlands, for the sun on the corn in the *patrón*'s fields. "And I can play my fife again," I murmured.

"That's right," Miguel said, "you haven't touched that thing for a long time, have you? At least you hadn't when I got carried off the *Sonora*." He smiled. "When we get home, you can play in the *cantinas*."

"I'm still hungry." Tomás stood up.

"I smell onions," I said and picked up a crushed stalk where we were sitting. I nibbled. It was strong but good. I ate it all.

We put on our clothes, almost dried in the blessed sun, and ambled along an Indian trail farther into the forest. Men from both ships were before us and after us.

Carlos set us to gathering everything that might be used for food. Antonio brought wild celery; Miguel found marjoram, over which Carlos rejoiced. Tomás and I dug large bulbs that looked like potatoes. Carlos

tasted them and said they would be good in stews. He'd
seen Indians eat these.

When we started back to the beach, Miguel made
signs to Tomás and me to fall behind. He jerked his
head toward the largest tree I'd ever seen.

"See how it towers over everything in the forest?"
Miguel whispered. "See how many wild onions grow
around it? Mark this place. Here's a spot we can't mistake or forget. When we escape, we'll meet here."

Tomás and I agreed it was a good choice for our rendezvous. Beside the massive tree were ferns, thick and
tall, to hide us from pursuers. We were as one about
the meeting place, but Tomás and Miguel argued about
the time for escape. Miguel wanted to try it the next
day; Tomás didn't.

"Don Juan plans to stay here a week," he declared.
"Could we keep out of sight for seven days? The time
for escape is the night before the ships sail. If Don
Bruno's eager to leave, he won't waste time searching
for us."

Miguel protested, then gave in.

"I had a picture of leaving at once, but you've a point.
I, Miguel, who do not like to bow to another's wis-
dom, agree."

He got busy with details. "Tomorrow Don Bruno
will take possession of this land in the name of the King;
then he'll put us to work. *Ai!*" he groaned. "I'd thought
never again to labor for the cursed Spaniards but—yes,
do not shake your head, Tomás—I know you're right."

That night we ate stew rich with herbs and green

stuffs. I kept waking up later, dreaming of home. I found my fife and held it close. At home, I'd play at fiestas. I'd tell of the marvels I'd seen, and my tunes would sing with happiness at being again with my own people.

Early next morning Don Bruno marshaled his men and made ready to take possession of the new land. The officers in their dress uniforms joined the two priests from the *Santiago,* who waited on the beach with a large cross built by the carpenters.

The cross was to be erected on the summit of the cape around which the vessels had sailed when they entered the harbor. A trail mounted the steep hill, which must have served as a lookout for the Indians.

Many had gathered from other villages to watch, and though they seemed friendly, Don Juan took no chances. On both ships seamen were left on watch, and armed sentries were stationed along the trail. I got in line with those behind the cross.

As we tramped up the trail, I was puffing before we reached the flat top, where the carpenters had built a small arbor. It was a clear day and we could look far out on the endless ocean. I wanted to see the land behind the hill. As we mounted I peered through the bushes and saw another beach to the north of the cape. Little bays and rocks lay offshore, and forest stretched toward distant rolling hills.

This land had plenty of places in which to hide, but once we got away, we would have a long way to walk.

I brought my thoughts back to the present. We stood

in square formation, facing the arbor and the cross. Father Campa commenced the mass. We were very solemn in this wild place, sea gulls flying overhead, naked Indians staring at us from all sides.

Don Bruno stepped to the foot of the cross and in a loud voice began, "In the name of the Holy Trinity . . ." I listened as he recited the circumstances of our arrival and proclaimed the land discovered for all time in the name of His Majesty, Don Carlos, King of Castile and Leon. The commander laid his hand on the sword in his belt, drew the blade and swished it at trees, grass, and rocks and asked all to witness that this place now forever belonged to Spain.

Was this how my country had become Spain's? The Indians didn't know what was happening, but I did. I wondered what these savages thought of all this. When a salute boomed from the guns of the *Santiago*, every Indian vanished into the bushes.

Before we started down the trail, Don Bruno made another announcement. "Since this is the feast day of Holy Trinity, we will christen this place Trinidad," he declared.

We moved quickly toward the beach. Gradually, the Indians came out of hiding, and Tomás mumbled that they didn't scare as easily as he'd thought.

Our holiday was ended and we went to work at daylight. At high tide the *Sonora* was run ashore, sea growths were scraped, and a mixture of hot tallow, sulfur, and pitch was smeared on her bottom. Tomás and I made faces as we worked. Tomás sneezed so much that Santana told him to get out.

"To the *lancha*, boy. I can't stand your sneezes."

I envied Tomás. Rowing back and forth transferring supplies was much better than this job. I tried to imitate Tomás' sneezes but couldn't. In the afternoon Don Juan summoned me to row the small skiff. As I rowed, he marked down measurements of water depth and the height of the tide. He wrote and wrote. Since I knew the pilot kept records, too, I dared a question.

"Do you and Don Francisco write the same things, sir?"

He smiled. "No two people see in the same fashion, boy. Besides, in the hazards of the sea, we must ensure that one record survives, even if one is lost."

I looked hard at him. He always seemed scornful of danger. Did he just ignore it? Don Juan's goal was the faraway unknown which the King had set. How many times our officers spoke about the importance of this expedition. All right, I thought defiantly. It's important to Spain and the King and our officers. Not to me.

Twice Don Juan took me with him to the Indian village. He was better than any of the other officers at making himself understood to the savages. I wondered if his interest in the way they lived helped him. I trailed after him as the Indians showed us through their square houses with the round doors.

"I wonder how they keep warm in winter." Don Juan mused. He made motions patiently until the Indian guide seemed to grasp what he wanted to know.

The savage bent over the pit in the center of the clean-swept earthen floor, squatted, shivered, then jumped up and threw a skin cloak over his shoulders, beaming up at Don Juan, who nodded.

"We might learn some tricks from them about keeping warm on the schooner," Don Juan said.

Not me, I thought. *I* won't be on that old schooner when it leaves here.

"What about that hut?" Don Juan asked, pointing to an eighth dwelling, which stood apart. The guide quit smiling; he shook his head. He walked in another direction.

"Odd," Don Juan said. "They'll never let us in that hut, though they show us freely their other buildings. Perhaps they store valuables or special supplies there and don't want us to see them."

When I mentioned the eighth hut to Tomás and Miguel, they were sure it was a storage hut.

"Wonder if we could steal food from it for our journey?" Miguel said. "No, if they won't let the officers into it, they probably keep a pretty close watch."

Of us all, Miguel was best at making friends with the Indians, especially the younger ones. A toddler took to following him, chattering, until Miguel stopped to watch him shoot arrows at a mark two or three yards distant. Each time the small boy hit dead center.

"*Bueno! Bueno!*" Miguel shouted.

The lad understood the admiration and beamed. When he hit his target the next time, he, too, cried,

"*Bueno!*" Tomás and I howled to hear Spanish from that naked *muchacho*.

In every spare minute, Miguel, Tomás, and I plotted our escape. Each would go when he saw his best chance. It was unlikely three could slip away together.

"Tomás may go in the morning, I in the afternoon, Lazaro in the evening," Miguel warned. "It doesn't matter. We'll meet by the giant tree. By full dark we'll be together and can strike out."

At last—the day! The officers of the *Sonora* planned a final visit to the Indian village.

"That wailing I hear isn't from sorrow at our departure, is it?" Don Juan joked.

"No. For a death," Don Francisco told him. "They'll burn the body tonight or tomorrow."

"Burn the body?" Don Juan crossed himself.

So did I. My skin crawled at the thought of burning flesh. I sniffed, but there were only familiar scents of grass, herbs, trees, fish, sea, and roses.

In late afternoon most of us went ashore. I wondered if Miguel had his stolen musket. I had scraps of food I'd pilfered. Tomás had his twine and three fish hooks in a cache beside the giant tree.

I had no weapon but my knife, and neither did Tomás. That should be enough. Again I heard our officers talking about the Indians.

"There must be three hundred visitors camped at varying distances from the local village," Don Juan said. "They all seem friendly. Did you know our hosts are giving us a canoeful of seafood just before our ships leave?"

"Good. We can use it," Pilot Mourelle replied.

My chance for escape came soon after that, and more easily than I'd expected. I was sent to the stream with the last water party. We'd filled our barrels and were heading back to the ship when Carlos decided to get one last supply of greens.

"If all of us bring in something," he suggested, "we'll have plenty very quickly."

It was as simple as that. I pulled wild onions until no one was close to me. Then I took the onions, found my poncho with its store of food, and fled up the trail. No one called to me; no one noticed me. I might have been a ghost as I passed the big tree and burrowed myself a nest among the thick, tall ferns. I lay flat on my stomach, ignoring the bugs that crawled over me, trying to ignore my thudding heart.

Had anyone seen my flight? No. There was no sound of pursuing footsteps. I was free.

Chapter VII

I LAY without moving for a long time; then I listened, hoping for sounds to tell me I was no longer alone in the forest. Where was Miguel? Where was Tomás? Had my absence been discovered? Were men searching for me? I reminded myself that it could be hours before Miguel and Tomás made their bids for freedom.

The ferns were high above my head. I sat up, putting my back against a fallen log. It was good to have something solid behind me. An object dropped on my head. I jumped and covered my mouth to smother a yelp. I looked at the ground. Only a twig. How Miguel would laugh at me.

I didn't stir until my legs were cramped and my back ached. I pulled away vines and ferns and stretched out flat. That was better.

Time dragged. The forest no longer seemed silent. Small animals scurried about me; a bird whirred over my head. Was that an Indian? I rolled over, peering, but the shape I'd imagined human was only a tall bush, the wind ruffling its leaves. Stop being a coward, Lazaro, I scoffed. When Tomás and Miguel come, you'll forget your fears and brag that you were first to escape.

I was hungry. I fingered my poncho and finally extracted a bit of salt meat. I ate it, finished off with a piece of cheese, then wished I hadn't. I was thirsty. I pulled up a nearby onion, wiped off the dirt and chewed it. I was still thirsty. I closed my eyes. If I went to sleep, which of my friends would waken me?

I don't know how long I slept. I wakened in blackness and knew that full dark had come. Thirstier than ever, I ran my tongue over dry lips and dared a whisper.

"Miguel? Tomás?" Perhaps they'd missed me in the darkness.

No answer. How long since I'd escaped? I had no idea. With luck, Miguel had said, we might not be missed for hours.

Again I shut my eyes, for I didn't want to look at shadows. Suppose Indians or Spaniards crept upon me? Or wild animals? I'd seen nothing but small creatures, but Pedro said there were deer, bears, and mountain cats in the forest. I listened fearfully until I once more fell asleep.

When I woke for the second time, daylight streaked through the trees. I sat up. Morning—and I was still alone. Had Miguel and Tomás gone on without me?

Were the ships gone, too? Surely Don Bruno wouldn't delay sailing to search for three boys. I was so thirsty my tongue felt swollen. I was afraid to go to the stream. What creature, wild or human, might see me? Loneliness overwhelmed me. If only Tomás or Miguel would come! I thought of Father, who'd sent me in his place. Had I betrayed him when I ran away? I tried not to think about it.

The searchers came at midday. Once, six of them were so near I could see their muskets and hear their swearing. I couldn't decide whether they were looking for one boy or three.

Need for water became stronger than fear. If I stood up, I might be shot before I could speak; even if I were not, I'd be hauled back to the ship and beaten with gun straps. Miguel and Tomás might be in the rope lockers now.

Every minute of that long day I expected to be captured, and after a while I was so thirsty I hardly cared. No sign of my friends! Perhaps they were dead.

At full dark I could no longer still my twitching body. I must have water. No matter what happened, I must drink. I crawled to the stream, knelt, and sank my face into the water, drinking until I could hold no more. Then I found a place to look at the harbor. The ships were there. I saw lanterns. Were searchers looking only for me or for the others, too?

I was not far from the Indian village. Miguel and Tomás might have hidden there. I remembered how friendly Miguel had become with the family of the small bow-and-arrow expert. What about that eighth hut? Miguel believed it to be a storage place. He could have gone there to hide. It was worth a chance.

When I reached the village, no one was in sight. I remembered the dead man; everyone must be at the funeral. I shivered, for in this lonely night it was not comfortable to think of the dead. I thought I could reach the storage hut without being seen. Even if I didn't find my friends there, it would be a good hiding place.

I scrambled into the hut by the round door, stood up and blinked. How could Indians stand so much smoke? My eyes smarted, my nose itched.

Then I saw it, emerging from the smoke with an awfulness that fixed my feet to the earthen floor. I was in a hut with a dead man. He was burning, but the fires must not have been lighted long, for his body was not charred. In the smudge and flames he looked alive. I stood there an eternity and beyond. Then a shift in the smoke or a draft through the hut sent the stench of searing flesh directly at me.

I fell to my knees. I was too terrified to shout, but choking moans came from me as I crawled and clawed through the round door. I was outside. I tried to run, but the ground came up to meet me and the sounds of my own fear died.

When I came to my senses, Indians surrounded me. The chief bent over me, grabbed my arm, and jerked me upright, talking crossly all the time. I tried to hang back, but he pushed me, waving his arms. I understood that he wanted to be rid of me. He released me and made shoving motions. The others copied him. The chief pointed toward the beach. So did his companions. Their expressions puzzled me. Why, they were afraid! Of me? No. Don Juan or Don Bruno, searching for me, must have accused the savages of helping me.

"I'll go back," I said. They didn't understand, but I felt better to have the words spoken.

I moved toward the beach. The Indians fell in behind. The chief gave me no time to hesitate. Men shoved a dugout canoe into the water, and I was thrust into the tipsy craft and paddled toward the schooner. When I stepped on board, Don Juan faced me.

"All right, Bo'sun," he said.

Santana grabbed my arms, faced me about, stripped away my shirt, and tied my hands about the mast. I bent my head. As I did so, I saw Tomás. He was free. He hadn't been beaten. Why, he'd never run away at all! Maybe Miguel hadn't, either. I, fool that I was, had been tricked by their fine talk of freedom.

The gun strap swished.

"Not yet, Bo'sun." Don Juan stepped closer, his gaze accusing. "Lazaro Sanchez," he said, "you have delayed the departure of His Majesty's fleet. Because of you and your companion in treason, our men have been forced to search Trinidad. Because of you, Don Bruno seized and held two Indians, keeping them aboard the frigate all day. Even though this endangered our friendly relations, this was necessary. By returning you to us, the Indians have absolved themselves of guilt, but Miguel

Rodriguez remains uncaptured. Before you are justly beaten, will you tell us where he is?"

Even in my terror I realized that Tomás had not been mentioned. He had preferred safety to freedom.

"Answer, Lazaro Sanchez!" Don Juan commanded.

"I never saw Miguel."

My fear must have convinced him. He stepped back and motioned to Santana. "Five lashes, Bo'sun."

The gun strap came down, burning my bare back. I won't cry out, I vowed, but when the second lash came, I did. I was ashamed, but I couldn't help it. My own cries were drowned in wails from the dugout canoes. The Indians! Why should they care? Why should they yell, wail, scream, their laments clearly pleas that I be spared?

Again Santana raised the strap; this time Don Juan halted him.

"Have done, Bo'sun. If we cease, our savage friends may yet deliver our other fugitive. Release the prisoner."

Santana untied my hands, pushed me into the galley, spread a scrap of blanket, and rubbed tallow on my back.

"Fool!" he muttered. "If Don Juan were different, you'd be shot. Is it true you didn't see Miguel?"

"Never," I mumbled.

"Then rest and thank the saints for their mercies."

I lay there alone until in the middle of the night Tomás crept to me.

"I never had a chance," he whispered. "I rowed Don Francisco all day long."

"You were afraid!"

"Yes," he admitted, "but I would have tried if there had been a chance. There wasn't."

"A coward never sees a chance! Go away! Don't ever speak to me again!"

He fumbled for my hand. "Here, I stole the last of the raisins for you."

"I don't want anything from you."

At daylight, Carlos nudged me in the ribs. "Back to your pots, boy. We sail in an hour."

I did as I was told, speaking to no one. I looked hungrily at the trees and the land. It seemed to me I caught one last whiff of the fragrance of briar roses.

How I hated the sea! Before my escape, I'd had hope. Some day ... some time ... I'd said and believed I could run away. When did a dream become impossible? The pilot had asked that question of Don Juan. I had an answer now, lashed into me by Santana's strap. My dreams and my hopes were dead.

Chapter VIII

CARLOS scolded me often that morning, for my mind was on Miguel, not pots. Where was he? If the Indians had been hiding him, they'd have taken him back, too. I wondered if Miguel had been delivered to the frigate while I slept, but Santana said no.

"He's still missing, Lazaro."

I pictured him clawed to death by a mountain cat, or fallen from a cliff, lying helpless and bloody on the ground. It wasn't fair! All Miguel and I had wanted was freedom.

He wasn't dead, though. Shortly after ten o'clock that forenoon, we saw a canoe put out from shore toward the frigate. Even from that distance I recognized Miguel's bright hair as he was put aboard the *Santiago*. At least, he was alive. He'd be whipped, of course. Would the Indians plead again for mercy?

The ships lifted anchor. As the schooner drew away from shore, I looked back with longing for the good solid earth. We were on a westward course. Who knew when we'd touch land again?

At first we had sunny weather; then, on the twenty-first of June, fog was upon us. For nearly eight hours we couldn't see the frigate. The *Sonora* fired guns to keep in touch. Whatever I was doing, I stopped and listened for the answering salutes of the *Santiago,* and always sighed with relief when they echoed across the water.

For two days we blundered through mists, then the sky cleared and the wind freshened. We were no longer at the end of the towline, for the schooner moved faster since she'd been worked upon at Trinidad Bay.

"Still, we may find ourselves on that towline again," Santana predicted. "It will be rough in these swells, but we can't go on losing ground every hour."

The officers talked about lost altitude and hard-fought northing, which meant that instead of progressing farther north, we were being pushed back. We communicated with the frigate only through signals, and what had happened to Miguel was still a mystery.

Eight days after we'd set out, the carpenter put our new topmast in place. He'd been busy at it ever since we sailed, and I often watched him work. The schooner responded, too, and as her speed increased, Santana bragged that we were now sailing better than the frigate.

We scudded along under great masses of gray clouds.

"They can't believe their eyes!" Pilot Mourelle declared, when mariners from the *Santiago* watched us. I was beside Don Francisco, but he ignored me. He had ever since the Indians returned me to the *Sonora*, and I was sure my whipping wouldn't have stopped when it did had he been in command.

I stared back at the frigate. Wasn't that Miguel at the rail? Yes, I couldn't mistake that burnished hair. Tomás edged up to me.

"That's Miguel!" He pointed.

"I see him."

I answered when Tomás spoke to me, but I never began a conversation and never sought him out.

"Who would have believed our snail would sail like this!" Don Juan was exultant. "Still, let us live with caution."

We sailed at a crazy angle, tipped to one side, and I understood why everything must be lashed down. All that bracing and roping served a purpose, after all.

We headed north in uncertain weather. We went from fogs to calms to windy tossings. Days became longer, and on the fifth of July, we had only four hours of darkness. The ocean was a strange world, with long sunrises and sunsets. Nothing seemed natural to me.

Three days later Don Bruno signaled that we must head for land, for this northwest gale was too much. The sooner I saw land the better. I was never dry, never warm, always tired. On the morning of July 9, Tomás came to me in excitement.

"I saw land!"

"You're imagining it!"

"No! See those mountains?"

"No, I can't. You're too anxious to see land."

By that afternoon we forgot about the coast, for we were caught up in a storm, a northwest gale churning the ocean to foam. Great waves pitched us about and broke over the deck.

"Holy Mother, we're done for!" cried the carpenter.

"We'll never weather this," men muttered.

"Lazaro!" Carlos yelled, and as the *Sonora* was sent on her beam ends by a fresh gust, I hurried to the galley.

I braced myself. There was an ominous crack over my head. At any minute we might plunge to the bottom of the sea.

"The new topmast's sprung!" Santana shouted.

Men were struggling above me. Waves crashed over us. The schooner was on her side, and I lay in the hold, water and spilled food sloshing around me. I couldn't stand. Something hit me. I thought the sea was rushing in. We were done!

I expected to be swallowed up in water, but instead I found myself in a sea of *garbanzos*. A bale of them had opened; they were around and under me. A barrel bumped me. Then the *Sonora* gave a heave and righted herself. Beans, onions, and enough rice for a dozen Sunday puddings swirled in a vast puddle.

The schooner rose out of the sea. I scrambled up as the cask rolled away. Water trickled down the side planking. I shook myself like a wet and dirty cat as Carlos careened into me, swearing and picking *garbanzos* from his wet shirt.

"To work, boy," he cried. "Save the food! It's all we've got."

Rice, onions, beans—the lot must be picked up and washed.

"We can't lose one ounce of corn," Carlos admonished. "Bad enough when we went on short rations a week ago."

For once he was down on his hands and knees doing some of the dirty work himself. That was what hunger did to a man. A few minutes later Don Juan came below and found me chasing beans under the cargo, scooping them into a copper pot.

"Good," he approved. "Save any morsel you can." He inspected the casks with concern.

Now I knew what had hit me and that the water had come not from outside but from our largest water cask, the one used as a reservoir. It had been almost full. We'd lost two others, the barrels still banging around noisily with each lurch of the ship.

For all its careening, the schooner's stout hull hadn't picked up much water except that spilled from our own casks. But this was a calamity. We needed every drop of it to drink.

"Things could have been worse," Don Juan told Carlos. "True, the mast is sprung, but we'll manage until we make land. By the color of the ocean, we must be near the coast. A rail, some hatch covers, and chocks were swept overboard, that was all. We didn't lose a man, and we've got all our canvas. We took the sails in before that blow could tear them to shreds."

I heard him, but all I really cared about was how close we were to land. When I went on deck, I doubted that we were near enough to set up a cheer. The others felt that way too. We'd all taken a beating in that blow; now that the gusts were over, we had our bruises. That barrel had given me a head welt, and my legs were scraped raw. I thought how tired I was after hours of chasing spilled food, and wondered how our officers could debate so hotly over that cursed French map.

"If there's truth in it," Don Juan said, "We ought to be sighting the strait discovered by Juan de Fuca in 1592. Was there ever such a fellow?"

"I doubt it. And if so, how could he have sailed these waters only a hundred years after Columbus discovered the continent?" Don Francisco said.

"The English believe in Juan de Fuca," Don Juan mused. "Not that I trust them much more than the French map."

"Somebody invented that strait," Don Francisco remarked gloomily, then grinned at his companion. "But if we find it, Juan, we'll put it on a map that's dependable."

Even the pilot said *if*. The question of when—and if—we'd return never left my mind. What about food for the journey? Living on mildewed *garbanzos* and dirty rice wouldn't be pleasant. We could get other supplies from the frigate—if we didn't lose her. She was out of sight much of the time when we scanned the horizon.

"I told you I saw land," Tomás said. "Look at the fish and ducks in the water. Look at those orange-heads!"

"I'll believe it when I see it!" I had to admit, though, these were promising signs.

All that night we sailed. It was noon the next day when the lookout cried, "Land, ho!" and all of us rushed to see for ourselves.

The country was nothing like that around Trinidad Bay. Don Francisco said the nearest point was forty leagues off. We saw a high range of snow-capped mountains with dark forests on their slopes. The frigate was on the far horizon, in the lee of the land, and when we tried to follow her in, the ebb tide carried us out. Don Juan looked worried.

"We can't approach the *Santiago*, yet we mustn't allow ourselves to be separated from her."

I thought of our sorry food supplies. If we lost the frigate, we'd starve. I watched anxiously as the ships signaled back and forth, and sighed with relief when the frigate decided to lie to and wait, since it was agreed the schooner shouldn't buck the high seas. The *Santiago* did wait until a new blow came up and she had to move out in late afternoon.

"Won't we get ashore, after all? I asked Santana.

"Sooner or later," he assured me. "Don Juan doesn't want to lose his topsails."

For two days we rolled, tossed, plunged, and finally had to put out into the open ocean. We were now a good five leagues from the frigate, and in those currents we'd have a hard time getting closer. Was this to be another Socorro Island, where we'd never get ashore?' Now it was even more important that we get fresh water and more food.

It made me uneasy to listen to our officers, as they worked on their charts and marked in several small islands, one of which they called Dolores. I could see it in the distance. Don Juan tried to signal the frigate and received no reply. What would we do if the *Santiago* deserted us?

Few slept that night. We sent up rockets and boomed cannonades. No answer. Tomás edged up to me at breakfast.

"The frigate's abandoned us to starve."

"I know that as well as you," I snapped.

Santana clucked dissent. "Neither of you knows that the *Santiago*'s really left us, and we'll make for land before we starve."

"We'd be wrecked on the shoals before we got there!" Tomás insisted, and there was a murmur of agreement from others who listened.

"Get out of here, boy!" Santana raised his fist. "If you can only croak about shipwrecks and starvation, talk to yourself." When Tomás scuttled off, Santana shook his head at me. "That boy wouldn't be so troublesome if you'd be friends. You'll have none of him. Why?"

"That's my business," I retorted and ducked before Santana decided to use his fist on me.

The frigate came in sight at noon the next day, but by that time the schooner had a worried, bad-tempered crew. Perhaps Don Juan longed for action, too, because he remarked that the roadstead looked guarded at either end by headlands, and why not go in behind that island?

The pilot agreed. "We need water. Perhaps we can find food, too."

We sailed into our haven and were immediately disappointed, for one minute the lead line showed eight fathoms, the next Antonio signaled only three. Then we were in the shoals, helpless and swaying with the tide. The pilot groaned that the schooner's bottom could spring open any second.

"Take the skiff, Francisco," Don Juan ordered. "Go to the frigate and tell Don Bruno our situation. Pray that the *Santiago*'s only on the other side of the cape and not beyond our reach."

Pray! I couldn't think of words. I was even glad to have Tomás beside me, though we didn't speak. It was late afternoon now. Low tide was around seven. If we couldn't leave then, we wouldn't dare to sail among those reefs in darkness.

"How long before tomorrow's high tide, Santana?" Tomás asked.

"Almost eighteen hours."

An eternity. We could be in eternity by then. When the pilot's skiff disappeared, we were truly alone, gulls and terns screaming above us, breakers crashing on the beach half a mile away. The jagged points of the rocks at the base of the nearest cape were like savage teeth bent on destroying us.

Don Juan made turn after turn around our tiny deck, dodging ropes and booms, checking our anchors.

Sunset came and with it a shout from the lookout. Indians! Canoes emerged from the mouth of a small river. These Indians were different from those at Trinidad. Lighter in color, they were stocky and muscular in cloaks of matting or furs. Shells hanging from their ears glistened in the waning light.

"I counted sixty canoemen," Tomás said.

We had eight seamen, some of them sick in the hold. If the savages attacked, we were dead men. They came closer, holding up freshly caught salmon.

"The key to the trade chest, Lazaro," Don Juan ordered. "Fetch the top parcel, the one with beads, knives, and mirrors."

I ran to obey and watched as the trading went quietly. The visitors smiled. Some held up sea-otter skins, gesturing that they wanted knives in exchange. I passed mirrors into eager hands.

The Indians seemed pleased, but they kept pointing at our anchor and waved, as if inviting us to visit their *rancheria*. Don Juan tried to make them understand that he'd visit them some other time.

All of us were glad when the savages went away. There were too many of them and too few of us. Don

Juan told Santana to make sure that every man had a musket at hand.

Muskets wouldn't be much good to us, I reflected, if these Indians swarmed over the *Sonora*. We were a poor handful for defense.

When sunset came, I found myself thinking that the color was like blood, and then at nine o'clock back came the canoes, every savage brandishing a weapon, every one howling. They sounded like evil spirits.

Don Juan handed out arms and assigned positions. He gave me a musket.

"Can you handle this, boy?"

"I've watched the others."

"I'll show you." He instructed me as the savage cries rose higher. Again he put the musket into my hands. "Don't make rash moves," he warned. He raised his voice so that all might hear. "Do nothing unless I signal. I don't like this late visiting hour. We must be ready."

We were tense as the canoes drew alongside, then Carlos bellowed with laughter and all of us gaped at him.

"Fish! Not war clubs! Fish!"

So it was. They had some women along, too. What we'd thought weapons were halibut, smelt, whale steaks, and venison. Carlos gloated as each item was given to us, but as for me, I eyed the bladders filled with spring water and baskets overflowing with sweet wild onions. I gripped my musket, but I could hardly wait for my turn at the water and onions.

Don Juan allowed three Indians to board the *Sonora*. He drank from a bladder, then passed the treat. How wonderful that fresh water tasted! We drank and drank and the savages laughed as they watched us.

"Put down your weapons and bring the trade goods again, Lazaro," Don Juan told me and smiled.

Now he gave out rings and earrings and necklaces, and the Indian women preened and exclaimed as they adorned themselves.

One squaw tried to hang an earring from her nose.

We ate and drank when we had a chance, but we were glad when Don Juan tried to make the savages understand the visit was over. They paid no attention. Canoes circled the schooner; heathen chants never stopped. Even when our three guests left the *Sonora*, the performance went on and on. We could hardly believe it when the canoes finally headed for shore.

Carlos and I were busy in the galley when we heard Don Juan talking to Santana.

"Pilot Mourelle ought to be back by now," Don Juan said.

Had something happened to him? Other savages out of our sight might not be like our friendly visitors. Everyone was relieved when the pilot returned at midnight.

"There's no haven south of the cape, Juan," he said. "That's what you wanted to know, wasn't it? Don Bruno has called another council meeting. He's talking again about sending us back," the pilot warned.

"I can't argue while we're on this reef." Don Juan's voice was edged with irritation. "How are things on the frigate?"

"Hardly a man is well and the commander himself is ailing."

I tried to sleep, wondering what was to happen. At daybreak we hoisted sails, but couldn't move, for the tide ebbed farther and the schooner swung with her bow toward the shoal. We were in a fathom and a half of water. The *Sonora* was plunging like a wild pony when the Indians returned, laden with furs. One canoe stayed near the rudder, the savages pointing and waving.

"They want iron," Don Juan declared. "That's why all those gestures about anchors and rudders. They've got their eyes on any metal that will make cutting tools."

He doled out more beads; he gave them barrel hoops and spare bits of metal. They weren't satisfied, though, and they left us without smiles or friendliness. Don Juan looked after them, then shrugged.

"We can't get out till flood tide," he said to the pilot. "Shall we go ashore for water? There must be a spring close by."

"Why not? We'll send the skiff."

I hoped to be in the shore party, but I wasn't. Santana was given five men, Tomás among them. Don Juan issued muskets, pistols, sabers, cartridge boxes, and hatchets and handed Santana a parcel of beads for gifts.

"Be on guard every minute. When you're ashore, send a man back with the boat to pick up the pilot and me. We'll bring the water casks. Find out where they can be filled in a hurry."

Tomás ran his hand over his musket. As he got into the skiff, he smiled at me and suddenly I hated to see him go. I remembered the times he'd tried to make peace with me. I thought of the stolen raisins I'd refused. I leaned forward.

"Tomás!"

He glanced up in surprise, for this was the only time since our quarrel that I'd spoken first.

"Yes, Lazaro?"

"Go with God, Tomás."

His eyes lighted up. "*Gracias.* I wish you were coming too."

"I wish I were."

We watched the skiff head for the place where the small river flowed into the sea at the foot of the high cape. Our men had trouble landing in the breakers; then they were over the skiff's side and wading, pushing the vessel through the surf.

"*Ai!*" Don Juan shouted. "Weapons! Keep your weapons—" His words were drowned in a roar from the shore.

One second no one was in sight except Santana's party; then Indians were everywhere. Brandishing clubs and waving spears, they swarmed from behind driftwood and exploded from the forest. Their howls rose above the breakers and the shouts from the schooner. Our men vanished in a wave of savages. We heard a single shot. That must have been Santana.

"No! No!" I cried. I yelled again, my voice lost as Don Juan fired the cannon. There! Indians wouldn't stand against cannon! But the shot fell short of its target and dropped in the sea, and the heathen didn't even notice it.

I lifted my musket, straddling the rudder to steady it. I saw a head bobbing in the water.

"Swim!" I cried. "Swim! Swim!"

It was Santana. No, it was Tomás! I didn't know who it was, but now two men were in the water. We shouted encouragement from the *Sonora* long after the heads disappeared.

Now only Indians were in sight. They fell on the skiff and ripped it apart, bits floating in the water. I wept, unashamed of tears scalding my cheeks. I looked at Don Juan, staring at the shore. Now only waves were on the beach. The Indians had vanished as swiftly as they had appeared.

Don Juan raised his fists. "They'll pay! We'll get the launch from the frigate! We'll revenge these murders!"

My own hands were fists. I burned for vengeance.

The tide was in and we could leave the reef, but we were short handed now. On deck were our officers, three seamen, and I. The others were too ill to work.

Before we could lift our anchors, we had an escort. Nine canoes bore down on us, at least thirty men in each vessel. The leading craft held nine, all armed with bows and arrows. Another Indian brandished a wooden spear tipped with a flint lancehead.

"Holy Mother, they'll kill us all!" Carlos muttered.

"We'll die fighting," Don Juan promised grimly. "Go below one at a time. Arm yourselves and return. Lazaro, stay at the rudder. I'll bring your weapon."

Pedro, in the masthead, sounded and watched for shoals. Carlos made cartouches; Felipe was to carry ammunition. Don Juan thrust a pistol into the sash about my waist and propped a musket beside me.

"You and I at the cannons, Francisco," he said. "Men, hold your fire unless the savages attack. If you fire, make every shot count."

How slowly we moved. Oh, for a swift ship! The Indians swarmed over our prow before we fired, then I shot into the face of a grinning tribesman, who'd only yesterday traded furs for knives. He toppled into the water and my stomach heaved. I'd killed a man. No! Only a murdering demon! I fired again. My second shot went wild. Cannons roared; muskets found their targets. We sought our way through the shoals.

The Indians fell back. One canoe was crushed by cannon fire. The men who'd boarded the *Sonora* fled. More gunfire! More howls! Then the canoes were paddling toward the river and around the long point. The battle was over.

Pedro yelled, "Here comes the launch from the frigate!"

Don Juan, his eyes blazing, took count. We were all there. Only Santana's party was gone forever.

Santana, Tomás—one by one I mouthed the names.

They must be dead. I hoped they were dead, instead of being tortured.

Don Juan's furious gaze met mine. I read in his eyes my own hunger for revenge. Why, he felt as I did! For the first time I thought of him as *my* captain.

Chapter IX

ON the *Sonora* we'd seen the massacre, but those from the *Santiago* could hardly believe it, for they'd thought our cannonades only signals that we were aground. They had brought cables to tow us from the rocks.

Don Juan assigned the watch aboard the schooner to sailors from the frigate and ordered Pedro and me to take him to Don Bruno.

"I'll lay this before the council," he said grimly and I knew "this" was a plan for revenging our dead comrades.

"Will we go with the party that hunts down the savages?" I asked Pedro.

"What party? Me, I'll wager Don Bruno sends no crew to be killed. Not when the Indians outnumber us by the hundreds. "

When we boarded the frigate, I saw Miguel, thinner, but grinning with his old brashness. As soon as the officers were in their meeting, Miguel crooked his finger and led me to a spot where we could hear what went on. We couldn't see the speakers, but voices carried through the open door to the officers' quarters.

"Miguel," I whispered, "Tomás was butchered."

"I know. But if we try to go after his killers, we may die, too."

We heard Don Bruno echoing this view. "I can't give you the launch and thirty men, Don Juan," he said. "Campaigns of vengeance are risky."

"But if those savages aren't punished, no white man will be safe on this coast!" Don Juan argued.

"We must think of our own, not those who come after. You killed six Indians. You lost six men. The score's even."

"Some of my six men may still live. Would you abandon them to torture?"

"We'll take a vote."

Miguel nudged me, whispering that every officer on the frigate would vote against a fight. "We'll go on, but you on the schooner will be sent back to Monterey. Oh, if I had stayed on the *Sonora!*"

He told me while we waited that Don Bruno had been ashore early in the morning and taken possession of land on the south side of the cape in the name of the King.

The officers were still arguing, and the suggestion of

turning back was put forth. Surprisingly, Pilot Perez spoke out.

"Since the *Sonora*'s come this far, I'd be the last to doubt she could go farther."

Voices faded, as speakers turned their heads or moved away from the door. Our officers had been determined to continue, and when Pilot Perez backed them, Don Bruno gave in.

"What about men to replace those I lost?" Don Juan asked.

"I'll give you a bo'sun's mate and five sailors."

"I'll be one of the five!" Miguel whispered. "You'll see."

He was right, and I wondered if he'd changed since he'd failed to escape. I couldn't tell.

By three that afternoon men and provisions had been shifted from frigate to schooner, and we set out in a rough sea. A gentle southeast wind rose, and for a week we steered west to get away from the land. One dead calm followed another, and twice our water rations were cut.

On the nineteenth of July Don Bruno called another council meeting. While it was in session, Miguel and I helped to bring more provisions from the frigate. As we stowed the first lot in the longboat, Miguel told me that half the *Santiago*'s crew were sick.

"Maybe the whole expedition will go back now." He was hopeful.

Whatever the council decided, we sailed on for a few

more days. A frigate sailor told Miguel that only our officers had voted to continue.

"Don Bruno and Don Juan talked about the water shortage," Miguel told me. "Our captain claimed it would be a pity if the King had to send out another expedition just because of a few mouthfuls of water." Miguel licked his lips. "It's mighty important when you don't have it."

I said nothing. I wondered if he knew our officers cut their own water rations when ours were halved. Three days later, Don Bruno signaled that fourteen men were down; the next day two more collapsed and twelve showed weakness.

"Scurvy," Don Juan said, when he'd acknowledged the message. "If only surgeons knew what to do for it!"

His voice shook. I studied him, for his hands were trembling, too, and last night he'd eaten nothing. If he gave in, what would we do?

"Lazaro," Miguel asked, "do your legs ache? Is your mouth sore?"

"No."

"Don't you have to rub cramps from your legs when you get up?"

"No. Did you know we're at latitude forty-seven degrees, forty-two minutes? That's a lot closer to the goal the King set, Don Juan says, but he's bound to reach sixty-six degrees."

"Oh, be quiet," Miguel groaned. "We'll be lucky to stay afloat in this fog." He peered anxiously. "The *Santiago*'s so far to windward I can barely see her."

Again Don Juan signaled the frigate to wait; again we caught up. The wind freshened and at flood tide both vessels lay to, sails furled. At five that evening we set out, tossed and buffeted by rough seas.

"I can't see the frigate's lantern!" Miguel joined me at the tiller. Since the Indian battle I stood occasional watches, though I was still Carlos' helper. Some of our sailors from the *Santiago* were sick, and there were not always enough to go around.

Don Juan ordered the guns and rockets fired.

"Francisco, in your opinion, shall we lie to?" he asked.

"No use trying to get closer to the *Santiago* until daylight," the pilot replied.

All night the worry of losing the frigate gnawed at us, even the sick rousing to voice fears, for on such a small vessel there are no secrets.

Morning came, and the fog thinned to mist, but there was no sign of the *Santiago*. For a day and a night we didn't move, and only Don Juan refused to admit we'd lost the other ship for good.

"Land lies west-northwest," he declared. "Since Don Bruno will keep to the same course, we'll soon sight him."

Did he believe that? Did the pilot agree? Not another man aboard thought we'd ever again see the frigate.

Fog as dense as smoke was upon us, and with it came overpowering loneliness. The world was blotted out, and we seemed to be at the edge of the universe. Was anyone else alive?

In our cramped prison we fretted over small things,

quarreled over the tone of a remark or a fancied slight, and always thirst aggravated our tempers, for now we were reduced to two cups of water daily. We still caught little dribbles from the sails whenever it rained. Miguel was scornful and said it was like trying to empty the ocean with Carlos' spoon.

Pedro, who'd listened to us as he ate his meal, now spoke up. "The *Sonora* needs help from above." Of us all, he missed most not having a priest aboard. "If we hold a solemn mass to Our Lady of Bethlehem, she'll see us through."

"And will she boost our rations?" Miguel challenged. "Besides, who'll pay for the mass? Are you a rich man, Pedro?"

"Everyone must give something," Pedro insisted. "When we reach the goal set by the King, we'll be rewarded."

"Ha!" Miguel scoffed. "You think the King'll reward Lazaro and me? I'd trade my chances for a jug of water and a good meal right now."

"I'll talk to Don Juan," Pedro said stubbornly, and as a result of that talk, the mass was said, everyone giving something. I contributed my fife, Miguel threw in a lucky stone, the officers gave coins. Even Miguel was impressed when we got favorable winds that afternoon.

"We should have spoken to Our Lady sooner," he declared.

Pedro frowned at him. "Do not joke, but I agree

we should have appealed to her before we were separated from the frigate."

His words chilled me. As our little schooner struggled in the slate-gray water, I had the feeling that even our words were hollow and echoing. I remembered going into a cave into the highlands. Just so did our words sound there. The *Sonora* was a cave, too, our only refuge on this vastness of water. How long would our cave last?

As I passed the officers' cabin, I glanced in and saw Don Francisco move quickly and put his arm about Don Juan's waist. He lowered our captain to his bunk.

"Lie quiet, Juan."

He was ill! I watched anxiously. In a few minutes he sat up.

"I'm all right." He sipped the wine the pilot brought him, and gradually color seeped into his white face. I wasn't deceived. He was as bad off as any mariner on the ship. How long could he hold out? I had a nightmare vision of Pedro, Miguel, and me, the last ones, trying to keep the *Sonora* afloat. If the frigate ever found us, how many would be alive?

I slipped away to help Carlos. I longed to tell someone what I had seen, but I didn't. When I served the officers that evening, I glimpsed a different expression on Don Francisco's face. They stopped talking when I appeared, but I sensed they'd had a disagreement.

"Pedro," I asked later, "if our officers had a falling out, what would happen?"

"That's ridiculous. They don't."

"But suppose Don Juan was ill and he wanted to

do something Don Francisco didn't want him to do—"

"Use your head, boy," Pedro retorted. "Don Juan is the captain. His ideas are the ones that count."

My fears were confirmed on the next day, when our officers argued about sailing to latitude 66.

"Use your head, Juan." The pilot was talking to Lieutenant Bodega the way Pedro had talked to me, as if he'd reached the end of patience. "Look at your French map! Land lies solidly to the north of us. To reach latitude sixty-six we'd have to pass around a large bulge of the continent."

"The King believed it possible when he ordered us to go there." Don Juan was stubborn.

"Has the King ever been in these seas?" Don Francisco flared. "What about the weather? Summer will be gone before we sail west far enough to turn into the Kamchatka Sea and the passage between Asia and North America. That's the only way we could ever reach latitude sixty-six. Your map tells us so."

"We are bound by duty to the King to go on," Don Juan said doggedly, then added that the continent was much larger than anyone had thought.

I knew then that Don Juan would not turn back. Nothing would sway him from his purpose.

Chapter X

WHEN I came on deck the next morning, we had a good wind. Pedro, at the tiller, sang praises to Our Lady, and Don Juan looked happier, too.

"In five days we'll have a full moon," he declared. "Our luck has turned."

I'd never looked at a full moon with such pleasure. The weather was clear and the breeze freshened. The *Sonora* sailed so well that Miguel exclaimed happily that we didn't need the frigate.

Land was ahead. We knew it from the color of the water, from the grass, orange-heads, and floating trees. We saw birds with red breasts, beaks, and feet. Their cheerful color seemed a good omen. We even saw a few whales, and Carlos said wistfully that whale steaks would taste fine.

"Hah!" Miguel scoffed. "You aim to spear a whale for us, Carlos?"

I knew a whale steak was impossible, but my mouth watered for fresh meat. I'd eaten the last of the sprouts from the shriveled and moldy onions and I longed for more.

Now, with the schooner sailing better, we were at 56 degrees and 8 minutes, but I sensed Don Juan's discouragement with our failure to find anything that was on the chart.

"According to the French map," he told the pilot, "we should be a few leagues west of an island. But who can trust the Frenchman's pen? My guess is that we're approaching uncharted islands, never seen by the Russians."

Charted or not, we sighted land at noon, six leagues away and slightly to the northwest. We all gaped at a mountain, proud above the others, with a symmetrical snow-white peak.

"Three thousand feet high," Don Juan estimated. "It isn't on the map."

I stared at the tree-covered shores, remembering Trinidad Bay, where Miguel, Tomás, and I had bathed in a stream and planned our escape. That was another world, another life, I thought, as I heard Don Juan christen the mountain St. Francis and the point of land extending from it, Cape Deceit. The peak was at 57 degrees 2 minutes. We were progressing. We were not yet defeated. I was cheered by Don Juan's improved appearance when Pedro and I rowed him to an inlet.

The north side was sheltered and deep enough, but there was no beach. We dropped anchor, but it dragged. Don Juan named the inlet Port Guadalupe, but Miguel muttered that it should be Muddy Bottom.

At dawn we moved out, and minutes later Pedro shouted "Indians!"

There they were, the first savages we'd seen since the massacre, and I think every man of us chilled with the memory of our last encounter. There were two canoes, with two men and two women, and I was glad when Don Juan ignored the savages' beckoning motions to go ashore. Our visitors didn't protest but went away and it was good to see the last of them.

The next morning we were in another port, with a fine beach and river. We anchored in six fathoms on a sand-and-ooze bottom, a gunshot from shore. High above us was a lone Indian house, surrounded by a pole parapet.

"We'll call this Remedios," Don Juan decided, "for relief is what we need. We must have wood and water, too," he added. "Keep your weapons ready and never relax vigilance for a moment."

At noon he sent five mariners to land on the opposite bank from the Indian house. The boat went back and forth, and some of our seamen had to be helped into and out of the vessel. On the fifth trip, I joined the fourteen already there. We kept looking at the Indian dwelling, but not a soul was in sight when Don Juan planted a cross and took possession of Remedios in the name of the King. Miguel and I carried muskets and the

Spanish flag, standing at attention while Don Juan read his words.

"In the name of the King..." Carlos III didn't seem a real person to me. I stood there thinking only of the goal he had set and that we might die before we reached it. In view of the silent fortification I was glad we had two cannons ready on the schooner as well as our armed guard on land.

We went back to the ship and scarcely had boarded it when the Indians rushed from their stockade, yanked up the cross and erected it in front of their house.

"Why do they do that?" Don Francisco asked.

"From their gestures I take it they mean to keep it there," Don Juan said. "Let them have it where they wish."

Close watch was kept on the Indians that night. Nothing happened, and the next day six of us went ashore on a point of land to fill the water casks. Don Juan accompanied us, repeating his warning to keep our weapons ready.

We were at the stream when twenty Indians left their stockade and marched to the opposite bank, gesturing and talking, halting now and then, as if expecting a reply.

"Wish I knew what they are jabbering," Miguel murmured.

So, I was sure, did Don Juan, but he made signs that we desired to be friends and wished only water to drink. The man who must have been the chief seemed to understand. He turned his head and gave orders, and presently men approached with a tightly woven basket filled with water, which they carried to the middle of the stream.

"Take it, Pedro," Don Juan ordered. "Give them beads and kerchiefs."

When Pedro obeyed, the chief fingered the beads, draped a kerchief over his arm and again spoke to his men. Presently we had another gift, this time of dried fish.

"That's better," Miguel whispered, "but still no water in our barrels."

Don Juan smiled at the Indians, then pretended to wash a barrel. The chief frowned and waved him away with motions that said clearly the water was theirs. We could drink; we had the gift basket. That must be all.

Again Don Juan waded into the stream while Pedro doled out more beads and kerchiefs. The chief watched and as soon as Don Juan swished the barrel there were shouts. The Indians bolted into their house and returned with stone-pointed lances, which they brandished.

"Ugly brutes," Miguel muttered.

Naked except for fur capes, they wore metal rings in their noses and shells in their ears. Some men had rings in their lower lips.

Don Juan spoke with decision, "We are not going to stand here all day. Do nothing to displease them, but we must have water and we're going to get it. Hold your arms ready. Don't fire unless I give the order."

He waded into the stream, musket in one hand, his

gestures plain. If the Indians tried to stop us, they'd be hurt.

Suppose they threw a lance at him. If he died, we'd all be butchered. But no. The savages suddenly retired to their stockade.

"Quick!" Don Juan urged. "Let us finish before they return."

We had never worked faster. We got our water safely aboard the schooner. Carlos and Pedro meanwhile had caught enough fish for supper. They tasted like haddock, Carlos said. He declared he could have caught many more if our tackle were different.

"Fish jumping all around us," Miguel grumbled, "and we can't catch enough to feed a baby. I wish the sun would come out. I've had a bellyful of fog and rain."

I, too, longed for warmth on my damp, cold body, but the fog and rain continued, and our thin clothes gave us little protection. Miguel came down with a cold. So did others. We could muster only two men for a watch and were glad when Don Juan, after obtaining wood and a pole for a mast, decided on the third day to leave Remedios.

"If we only had medicine and a surgeon," he said.

"Perhaps we'll be like Martin de Aguilar," Don Francisco said. "He found his river but didn't live to tell about it, so his discovery was no good to anyone."

Don Juan laughed. "We will *not* copy him. We'll go back to San Blas and our map will live long after we're dead." After a moment he continued, "But as loyal officers of the King, Francisco, we ought to try and see what the coast the Russians explored is really like."

"Loyal officers of the King!" Never had the pilot been so sharp. "Dead officers! And will that do anyone, even the King, any good?"

"Are you afraid to take a chance on dying?" Don Juan was scornful too.

"No! But I'm not willing to make a fool of myself to attempt to reach an impossible goal! We might as well try for the moon!"

"Are you calling me moonstruck?"

"Yes! And you're sick, too!"

There was silence for a long time. Later when I entered the cabin to tidy it, Don Juan was alone. He was running his finger over his map, lingering on the line marked, "Route of the ship *St. Peter*, commanded by Bering." I stopped and peered at the paper and the dim line. It twisted among islands to a cape called St. Elias and St. Elias Mountain. Don Juan looked up.

"Lazaro, Commander Bering was here in 1741, only thirty-four years ago. Wouldn't you like to see that mountain and that cape?"

"I suppose so."

I couldn't tell him outright that I didn't care if I never saw them. Don Francisco loomed in the doorway and I knew the words had been meant for him. He didn't mention Cape St. Elias when he spoke, just looked hard at Don Juan.

"It's the twenty-first of August. Now that we are

leaving Remedios, you surely aren't sailing farther north?"

Don Juan stood up. "Yes I am." He sounded angry. "I know what I am doing."

Don Francisco stalked off. On deck he looked unhappily at our wake as a brisk wind carried the *Sonora* farther into the unknown.

Earlier Don Juan had placed little confidence in the French map; now he was determined to learn the truth about it, seeking islands that were shown to the west of us in our present latitude. No islands appeared. All we could see was open ocean.

On the second day out of Remedios, at latitude 58, according to the quadrant, Don Francisco broke his long silence again.

"We're now farther north than Bering's sister ship, the *St. Paul,* sailed If we believe what the map says."

"Then soon we should see the great mountain in the distance," Don Juan declared.

"The one the Russans reported? Who knows how accurate their navigating instruments were? It may be far away."

"Isn't that what we're supposed to discover?"

Don Francisco discarded all pretense of politeness. "Aren't you satisfied that you've found a mountain of your own they didn't know about? Isn't that enough? If we don't turn back, we'll freeze in the Arctic or be lost in the autumn storms."

When Don Juan didn't reply, the pilot rushed on. "If you asked the men how they felt now, you'd get a different answer from the one you got last time. If you want any mariners alive to bring this schooner into her home port, you'd better act now or you won't be around to report what you've seen. Juan, can't you give up and admit you're sick?"

Don Juan looked away from his companion. "I see little hope of success if this is the way all of you feel."

"It is the way. I tell you as your friend. No matter that you find me quarrelsome."

"Then turn about. That is the way it shall be written in the log. I will not say that it was my wish. Only because of the men will I take this step."

After the *Sonora* reversed her course, Don Juan barely spoke to anyone, except to give orders. On the next day, however, I heard him say to the pilot that, even if we were not going forward, we were going to learn some other truths about this land.

"We're going to find the Strait of Admiral Fonte," he declared.

Pilot Mourelle held up his hands in despair, but I asked Pedro who Admiral Fonte was.

"Take your curiosity to the pilot, Big Ears," he advised.

I did just that, and to my surprise Don Francisco answered in a friendly way.

"He may have been another pretender who invented his exploits," he told me. "He reported finding an archipelago and a great strait between islands. He said he crossed the entire continent of North America in the strait. Another man with a great imagination, I say."

Later he repeated this remark to Don Juan, adding, "If Fonte's entrance exists, how could we have missed it? Haven't we rounded every headland, searched every bay and seen nothing? That strait's as much fantasy as the French map."

Don Juan was stubbornly silent, and the officers had another session on the next day when we found an arm of the sea with no end in sight and anchored a musket shot from shore.

"What if we went up that channel," Don Juan speculated.

"To explore it and see if it goes across the continent? Are you mad, Juan? Let it be enough if we go ashore and take possession."

Reluctantly Don Juan gave in and told Don Francisco to perform the ceremony. I went along, carrying the cross and keeping an eye out for Indians. We saw none, but we found a hut at the end of a beaten path and footprints leading to a wooden shed.

The place was to be named Bucareli Bay, in honor of the Viceroy, and the ceremony couldn't end fast enough for me. As soon as we took on wood and water, we'd bathe in the stream and see what food the land would offer. I'd have thought Don Juan would have had enough of being cooped up in that tiny ship, but when the rest of us went ashore, he lay in his cabin.

When our tasks were done, Miguel and I bathed and gorged ourselves on sweet, dark berries that grew in quantities on bushes. We gathered a pot of them for the galley, and I put a good supply into my poncho to take aboard and hide in my secret places.

Miguel, in better humor, grinned at me, as we feasted that night on venison and huckleberry pudding. Pedro had shot a deer close to our anchorage.

"Lazaro, I never saw anyone find so many places to hide food on such a small ship," Miguel said.

No one else did it, but I paid no attention to the ridicule. Even those moldy onion sprouts had come in handy.

We went ashore on the next day, too, reveling in the warm weather, eating fish that Carlos caught, gathering more berries. Don Francisco suggested that we stay several days, but again Don Juan was contrary. Now that the men seemed better, he wanted to push on with his explorations, and early the next morning we sailed. Our good spirits didn't last long when Don Juan gave a new order.

"We are all in better health," he announced. "I'm reversing the course. The wind is rising and ought to carry us to latitude sixty-six within a few days. Then we'll see the Russians' cape and mountain."

Don Francisco didn't try to hide his disgust. "You're the captain!" he said, and our officers didn't speak to each other for the rest of the day.

I crept about my tasks. I'd never known the *Sonora* to be so silent. No one had the courage to break the tension.

When Miguel relieved me at watch, he was shivering. "Every tooth in my head aches," he groaned.

"Want my poncho?" I asked.

He took it, but he still shook, and Don Juan, eyeing him with concern, spoke up.

"All of you need warmer clothing, don't you?" he asked. He was huddled in his own greatcoat, the one I'd carried aboard. "I'll fix you up." The old spark momentarily came into his eyes, and he was the old Don Juan, who'd rallied us to him.

"Francisco," he went on, "we never did use a lot of our trade goods, did we? The savages ran around naked or had fur capes of their own. It's in my mind that our men have greater need than Indians for the King's goods."

The pilot's glum expression lightened, and this time there was no argument between them. Except for the man at the tiller and the sick in the hold, the rest of us followed Don Juan as he explored the trade chest and brought out yards of warm flannel. He divided it in lengths.

"Sailmaker, sew these into shirts. Lend your needle to any who can handle it," he said.

My eyes strayed from the woolen goods to the four coats Don Juan drew from the box. One, an officer's, had big gold buttons and gold braid. Miguel nudged me.

"Wonder how that water-greedy chief would've looked in that?" he whispered.

I smothered a chuckle and Don Juan smiled.

"Put on the coat, Lazaro. Its owner must have been tall; it should come to your knees."

I slipped my hands into the sleeves and wriggled happily at the warmth across my shoulders. I didn't care when the crew hooted at me.

"Now if you only had a tricorn hat," Don Juan suggested.

We laughed together. Never again would I be afraid to remember that encounter. That night I heard the officers talking over their evening meal and guessed that the incident of the trade goods had smoothed out their earlier arguments.

We were happier that night, but our contentment was too good to last, for the next day we were in new storms and high seas, a gale howling in the rigging, driving us toward cliffs on shore. All of us who could stand struggled to claw the *Sonora* off the land in the brief lulls between squalls.

"*Dios mío!*" the pilot cried. "At times it would be a relief to abandon ship!"

A week ago Don Juan would have countered this; now he only worked silently. I dug my hands into the pockets of my fancy coat and found a few dried huckleberries. When I offered half of them to Miguel, he refused.

"My mouth hurts too much to eat those things."

I chewed and studied the others. All of us had lost weight. Don Juan's cheeks were hollow, his skin the color of moldy bread. His dress uniform would have fit him like a sack now. Pilot Mourelle's fair hair was dull, as if it were the white of an old man rather than blond. Pedro was almost as shaky and shivery as Miguel, whose face was pinched under his flaming hair. Carlos' elbows and wrists were sharp, as if his flesh had shrunk. I didn't even want to think about the others who were stretched out in the hold.

It was the first of September before the west winds blew and we could get away from the dangerous coast. We could carry only a little sail, for a gale was building up. That morning I helped Pedro from his blanket; his legs were swollen. He said three Hail Marys before he took over as my relief. His thanks were sour and he eyed me curiously.

"A real mariner on your first sea voyage, Lazaro. Holy Mother, it may be your last one, too."

I heard those words in my dreams and woke instinctively when I knew Miguel should be taking over from Pedro. I rolled from my nest, snugged my fancy coat about my throat and stuck my head out of the companionway. Don Juan was on deck. He glanced at the tiller.

"Where's Miguel?"

"I'll get him, sir."

"Do. I'll relieve Pedro until Miguel comes."

I had only to look at Miguel to know he would stand no watch. His legs were swollen from ankle to knee and his words were mumbled.

". . . can't stand . . . tried . . . can't . . ."

I made an effort to boost him upright, but it was impossible. I went back and reported. Don Juan's shoulders slumped. He looked at Don Francisco, who was about to go down and get some sleep.

"Our crew now numbers two. Three, if we count the cook."

"Plus you and me, Juan."

"And will you guarantee that both of us will be upright by tomorrow's dawn? All right, all right." He was bitter but resigned. "We'll turn about at once. I cannot fight all of you, as well as the hazards of the sea. We have gone as far as we can for the King."

Don Francisco stepped forward and put his hand on Don Juan's arm.

"Remember, Juan," he said gently, "we've been farther already than anyone else has ever gone."

"Not far enough," Don Juan retorted, but he gave the orders to reverse course in a steady voice.

In the morning Carlos was full of talk and fear.

"It is a long way to San Blas. What if the *Sonora* smashes against the rocks? What if we all die?"

"Santana would have said, 'Cease your croaking,'" I told him, but my hands shook as I ladled out the porridge. We had come a long way for the King. We still had all that distance to go home.

Chapter XI

THE storms died as we headed south, and we began to talk about what we'd do when we reached San Blas. Even the sick managed a few words, though I wondered if some of them would ever see San Blas. Gil, the quartermaster, was on his feet again, and Pedro could still stand watch. Sixteen seamen were crowded into the stinking quarters below deck, some of them so weak that Carlos or I had to hold them up to feed them.

The officers worked again on their charts, and several times they smiled at my interest and explained their findings.

Miguel, in his nest among the spare canvas, talked little, but once, when I brought him food, he kept staring at me.

"What's wrong?" I challenged. "Aren't you used to my gold buttons yet?"

He frowned, as if trying to straighten out something in his mind. "Lazaro, when we tried to escape, you hated the Spaniards as much as I did. Now you dog their footsteps like a bridegroom hurrying to his wedding. You flap your ears every time they draw a line on those cursed maps."

Had I changed? Why *was* I curious about the maps? Miguel prodded me.

"When we first sailed, Carlos or Santana had to cuff you into staying awake. Now you're on deck at dawn. Why?"

"There are so few of us."

"That's not the reason. If we ever get home to San Blas—"

"Forget San Blas," Pedro cut in. "Keep your mind on Monterey. That's closer."

"You going to ask Our Lady of Bethelehem to give us a tow?"

"Maybe I will," Pedro retorted.

If he did, Our Lady didn't come through, for at night new winds howled down on us, and when I staggered on deck, Don Juan was reefing the sails.

"Hang on to the tiller, Lazaro!" he shouted.

Waves crashed over the gunwale, rails broke, stanchion clamps and awning supports were swept overboard. Water poured over the hatch and into the hold. I heard frantic prayers from the sick as they tried to crawl to safety on top of casks.

Knee-deep in water, I clung to the tiller. The world was water and foam and terror. I stood in the ocean. No part of the deck was in sight.

"Lie to!" the pilot yelled. We were so close to shore the roaring breakers threatened. Gil fought to furl the remaining sails.

"Keep the prow headed south!" Don Juan cried.

We were sinking! I was sure of it! Then the *Sonora*, the unbeatable old tub, rose out of the churning ocean, and water poured off through the scuppers.

"Gil!" I yelled. Where was he? Had he gone overboard?

No! In the dim light of coming dawn, I saw him in the companionway, flat on his back, pinned down by a smashed rail across his legs. Pilot Mourelle rushed to pull away the debris and boosted Gil to his feet, guiding him toward the hold.

"Keep headed away from the coast, Lazaro!" It was the first time Don Francisco had called me by name. I felt good. Why, the *Sonora* depended upon me!

Presently the officers, wet and cold as I, joined me.

"Take the tiller, Francisco," Don Juan ordered. "I'll handle the sails. Lazaro, go and help Felipe and Pedro at the pumps. Carlos will try to do something for the sick."

Felipe had been down when this started, but now he was working with Pedro. As I went to them, I saw sick men lying high up out of reach of the water, the ocean still seeping in through closed hatches. The men looked more dead than alive, but I forgot them as I worked.

Bend and pull, bend and pull. The rammer of the pump clogged. We stopped to clean it. Bend and pull. Bend and pull. The cold was in my marrow. I couldn't stand. I had to. Bend and pull. Bend and pull.

"Lazaro!" It was Felipe, his face gray. "We're gaining. Tell Don Juan the water's dropped an inch."

"Sure?"

"Sure."

I staggered to report, but Don Juan hardly listened. He was watching the pilot, who leaned over the stern and worked feverishly on something out of sight.

"The gudgeon," Don Juan said. That was the metal pin let into the end of the wooden shaft of the tiller. "If it can't be repaired, we'll have nothing to steer with."

I gaped at him. A *Sonora* that couldn't be steered? Impossible!

Don Francisco had found a bolt in the remaining part and was trying it. "Juan, give me a hand. I think it's fixed."

Then Don Juan was tugging him upright. The expression on their faces told me that the schooner was once more in working order.

I went back to the pumps, and by eight the next morning we were watertight, with not a drop in the hold. That night we lay to. All who could helped to restore the vessel to some order. Miguel didn't move and even refused a cup of wine I brought to him. A half hour later, I found Don Juan in his bunk, his eyes closed. I touched his hand. His eyes opened, but he didn't move.

"Chocolate, sir?"

He shook his head and spoke painfully. "Can Felipe stand watch?"

"No, sir. He collapsed two hours ago."

"Pedro?"

"Yes, sir."

Don Francisco came into the cabin and spoke harshly. "Lazaro, are you and Pedro the only mariners upright?"

"Carlos is up and down, but he's busy with the sick and in the galley."

"Holy Mary! That I should live to see a cabin boy outlast a quartermaster and a bo'sun's mate!" When Don Juan tried to sit up, the pilot pushed him back. "Rest, *amigo*."

"The coast," Don Juan murmured. "If we could find another Bucareli Bay and could take our sick ashore . . ."

"Rest, *amigo*," Don Francisco repeated.

I went away. If Don Juan couldn't get up, what would we do?

He made it on deck that afternoon when we sighted land at 53 degrees and 54 minutes and feasted our eyes on islands. At 49 degrees we coasted along, staying a mile out from shore. The wind was more favorable. The sun came out. When I told Felipe, he crawled out, but when I tried to rouse Gil, he neither moved nor spoke.

The sunshine didn't last and new winds drove us from the coast. The next day we were in a northwester. I watched our officers anxiously, and saw that eating was a chore for Don Juan. The pilot was in the bunk now, and Don Juan, standing with difficulty, waved him back when he tried to rise.

"Your turn to rest, Francisco. We'll show ourselves one at a time, so that the men need not know their officers are ill."

I doubted that anyone was deceived, and Miguel voiced the feeling of all.

"Tomorrow we may be adrift, with no one able to stand. And in the next storm, we'll die."

"Not me!" I told him. "When we find the River of Martin Aguilar—"

"There never was such a river!"

"Only this morning we saw a cape shaped like a table. Aguilar reported such a cape near his river."

As I left Miguel, I wondered if we wished so hard to find the right cape and the right river that we imagined things.

Strong currents carried us south and there was no opportunity to take observations. Don Juan would have liked to correct the location of the cape on his map.

At 38 degrees he sent up a great cry.

"A river! The mouth of a large river! Steer into it!"

We tried, but it was easier said than done, for that evening we fought a violent tide until at last we cast anchor near a sandy point which Don Juan named Arenas. We were so exhausted that only Don Juan stayed excited.

"If it isn't a river, it's San Francisco Bay! I'm sure of it! Ayala will be there! It will be good to see him again."

Don Francisco grunted. "We could be miles from San Francisco, Juan. What makes you—"

Don Juan interrupted him with another shout. "Look! A wharf! San Francisco it is! Up anchor! Move to it!"

"But where are the people?" Don Francisco was still skeptical. "And where are the small islands supposed to be opposite the entrance?"

"And the mission?" Pedro said anxiously. "The one that was to be built last summer? Around missions there are always fields where grain and vegetables are grown."

I couldn't make out a wharf, only a light spot on shore, but I told myself Don Juan was usually right. I prayed that again he'd seen more than the rest of us. I wished I could stay on deck until we reached shore but because Carlos had collapsed again, I had to work in the galley, ladling out the breakfast, impatient as the men complained again about the weevily gruel. When I heard Don Juan exclaim, I dropped everything and hurried to deck. I stared incredulously at the shore.

There was no dock! What Don Juan had mistaken for a wharf was only a large point of rocks. This wasn't San Francisco. There was no mission, only a strange inlet.

Silence draped the *Sonora*. The only sounds were the slapping of water against the vessel and the moans of the sick below. Don Juan spoke.

"Rock or not, we'll go ashore. We'll moor and put our sick on land."

"For another massacre?" the pilot demanded. "We'd better find out what those savages are up to first."

There they were, paddling their reed canoes, staying away from us, crossing from one side of the harbor to the other, finally climbing a small, close-by hill to set up a chorus of shouts. Angry or welcoming? Who could tell?

"I don't see any weapons," Don Francisco commented.

The Indians were swarthy, stocky, and powerful. Don Juan studied them, then spoke with decision.

"We'll take a chance. Our sick will be better on land than in the hold. Stand by the cannon, Francisco."

Pedro and I carried Miguel, who opened his eyes when we laid him with the others on their ragged blankets spread on the rock.

"Good. If I must die, I'd rather do it here."

"Better not to die at all!" I scolded.

The Indians came with presents of feathers and bone necklaces, which no one cared about, but when they set down a large basket of ground nuts, we fell upon the treat. Oh, how good! Sweet, rich, and oily, they cut the taste in our mouths of the moldy ship's fare. When I popped nut meats into Miguel's mouth, he chewed slowly, then eagerly. Only Gil would take nothing and lay as still as a corpse.

"Get mirrors, kerchiefs, and beads, Lazaro," Don Juan ordered.

I held out the gifts, and wanted to laugh at the surprise on the dark faces.

"Their hairdos are fancy, aren't they?" Don Juan remarked. "Lazaro, ladies in Spain dressed their chignons like that, though I doubt that the ladies would appreciate the comparison."

I smiled, but I was glad when the savages left, for the memory of the massacre was too vivid.

When night came, Don Juan ordered the sick brought aboard and placed watches carefully. He took the first watch himself to give Pedro and me a rest. It was a pleasant, balmy night, unlike those in northern waters, and I curled up on deck, only a few feet away from Don Juan.

I listened to the night sounds; the sigh of the waves against the rock was different from their lapping against the hull when the *Sonora* was far out at sea. The noise of the men's snoring was comforting, but I kept straining to hear skulking marauders. I lay very still, huddled in my fancy coat, and presently Don Juan came over to me. When I sat up, he pushed me back.

"I sensed that you were not asleep, Lazaro."

"No, sir."

When he spoke again, it was in an intimate whisper that reached only my ears.

"You are not in despair because we have not yet reached San Francisco Bay?"

I had been, for when Don Juan had been deceived by a rock, I had given up all hope of ever seeing home again. Now, hearing an appeal in his tone, I answered carefully, ignoring the emptiness in me.

"If you say we'll reach home, I'll believe you, sir."

Again he was silent, then touched my shoulder.

"Good boy. Lazaro, I've often wanted to tell you that you brought me luck. First, your words sent me aboard the *Sonora*; second, your appetite spared you to become a valued mariner."

So he had known about my hoarded onion tops and berries.

"If anything prevents us from returning," he went on, "I wanted you to know my feeling. Regardless of a muddy hat and your running away, I am proud of the boy who gave up his fife for a mass and wore his gilt-buttoned coat with good humor. Now that same boy has put a needed brace on my own faith."

I was breathless. That Don Juan should say these things to me! I didn't sleep a wink the rest of the night.

I couldn't have, anyhow, after two o'clock, for a terrific high tide rolled in through the narrow mouth of the passage, and in seconds we were taking a pummeling, spray dashing high about us. Our small boat was smashed to bits, and even as the splintered wood flew about, Don Francisco groaned that there went our last chance to go ashore.

"We can't even return here to rest as we did at Bucareli Bay. Juan, now we must do with what we have until we reach Monterey—or the bottom of the sea."

He meant we couldn't leave the schooner even if it was sinking. Our last chance was gone, for now we couldn't even try to reach shore and make our way home by land.

"The cable's broken!" Pedro shouted. "And we've lost an anchor!"

Yesterday we would have despaired over these disasters; that night we had all we could do to fight going against the rocks. There were only four of us to keep the *Sonora* afloat, but our officers, Pedro, and I kept at it through the desperate hours of the longest night I'd ever known.

How narrow the harbor mouth! How could it have seemed wide when we first saw it? How savage the currents! Then morning came and with it a changing tide. We sailed with the ebb and were moving out when Indian canoes came alongside and handed up another basket of ground nuts. As I accepted the gift, I blessed them, and though they didn't understand me, they must have known the spirit of our thanks shouted from deck.

As the fog lifted, we saw a cape five miles off. We sailed on, keeping as close to shore as was safe.

In half a day the nuts were gone, and we were back to our scanty, moldy ship's fare. Our officers never appeared together, and I knew only willpower kept them going. At sunrise on our second day out, we saw islands, and Don Francisco raised the first cry.

"This time it *is* San Francisco!"

Pedro fell to his knees and prayed, but I could only stare, not daring to believe that soon we would be safe at a mission, with people who were well, who'd give us meat and bread, and—suddenly something about Don Juan halted my inner thanksgiving. What was wrong? Why was he sad? The pilot, too, wheeled to study him. Don Juan spoke slowly.

"To dodge shoals and rocks," he said, "we'd have to tack against contrary winds and tides. We'd have to breast a swift-running tide in the neck leading into the bay."

"But then we'd be in San Francisco!" the pilot cried.

"Can we risk it? We have no assurance of what we'll find there. Something may have happened to prevent the settlement from being founded. No, Francisco, with only only four of us to man the ship, we must go on to Monterey."

"But we could miss Monterey! It, too, is a small place in a large coastline."

Don Juan's knuckles were white on the rail. "It is the lesser chance." He lifted his head and spoke as lightly as if all our lives did not hang on this moment. "We've come this far. Surely with the help of Divine Providence we can sail on."

Pedro clambered awkwardly from his praying position, and I tried not to tremble as I held the tiller. We were all asking guidance from above. But would it come? Emptiness spread through me. I was a hollow gourd, not from hunger but from loss of hope. All our work, all those long days and endless nights, all the shifting of sails, the labor over the pumps, the beatings in storms, the terrible food were for nothing. We were doomed. I was sure from that moment.

Again I looked at Don Juan. I had told him only two nights ago, "If you say we'll reach home, I'll believe you." I had meant it then, but how could I feel that way now when I was so weak, I who had stood up longer than the rest?

Somehow we kept going. We had to hold the schooner

far enough off the coast to be safe from shoals, yet we could not risk getting more than three miles from land. Now I understood Don Francisco's despair when our small boat was smashed. If we still had it, we might have abandoned ship and walked the rest of the way.

Even managing the sails was an effort. None of us had the necessary strength, but somehow, working in pairs, we carried on. Then we struck a calm, and that night fog swallowed us.

Death seemed around the corner. We were so weak not a man on board expected to live through this. I wanted to get away from the others, to think of my mother and father and the home in the highlands I would never see again. Pedro told his beads over and over; sick men, lying on deck, mumbled prayers; even Miguel whispered that he wished he'd paid more attention to the priests.

I remembered the bad omens we'd had—how I'd missed the blessing of the fleet, how we'd changed commands when barely started. Maybe this was foolishness, but how can a person have either courage or hope when his belly growls with hunger and his legs wobble from weakness?

Where, behind this shroud of fog, was the sunny land of California? How could we have come this far, borne all we had lived through, only to fail a few leagues from our goal?

Despair settled on the ship. Another night dragged on.

Next day I was on noon watch, peering into the white

nothingness of the fog. Suddenly I saw a vision. Or was it?

Had the fog thinned? I blinked and looked again. It was true—the fog *was* lifting. And there before me was a distant indentation. I opened my mouth to shout, but my words came out thin and uncertain.

"Land! A point of land!"

They heard me—the officers, Pedro, and Carlos were beside me. Pedro spoke first, his voice cracked with unbelief.

"A ship! *Dios mío,* a ship!"

"Fire the mortar!" Don Juan croaked.

The pilot staggered to the cannon, and its sound boomed across the water. Birds rose, screaming into the misty sky. There was no answering gun. My heart sank. Were we all dreaming?

"Again, Francisco."

Pilot Maurelle and Pedro struggled to load another shot. The blast echoed, and more squawking gulls churned above us. The sick crawled from the hold, crying questions, but those of us who strained our eyes toward shore had no reply. We could only stare at that shadowy vision of a ship, still stationary beyond the point. It *was* real! It had to be.

Then our answer came. Boom! Boom! Boom! Oh, never in my lifetime will I forget it!

"The *San Carlos!*" Now Don Juan's voice was joyous and firm. "I'd know those guns anywhere!"

Chapter XII

WE lived! The miracle endured as longboats appeared
in the gentler mist and took the schooner in tow. Men
clambered aboard us with bread and fresh fruit. Pedro
and a frigate sailor hugged each other, tears rolling
down their cheeks.

Miguel crept out and clung to the rail. Everyone who
could crawl was on deck as the mission bells pealed a
welcome. Only when I saw Don Bruno boarding the
Sonora did I dare to believe our trials were truly ended.

On the next morning all of us were ashore at the
Presidio, our officers quartered in an adobe house, the
rest of us in sheds. Miguel, Pedro, and I were together;
within two days we were almost as good as new. How
we ate! The frigate sailors claimed we wolfed three

meals every time we sat at a table. We laughed and ate more.

Even Gil, worse off than anyone else, began to improve, and Pedro's friend told us that as far as the sickness was concerned we'd been lucky on the schooner, for three men had died aboard the frigate.

"When we lost you," the sailor said, "we turned back to the place of the massacre but could learn nothing. Later we passed what seemed to be a great river emptying into the ocean. But we were too weak to handle oars for exploring it. Don Bruno marked this place on the map and called it 'Heceta's Entrance.'"

"And after you reached Monterey?" Pedro asked.

"Don Bruno went by land to San Francisco, hoping for news of you, but there was none. Who'd have thought your little tub would continue north? Not even Don Bruno expected it."

Pedro and I exchanged proud smiles.

"You don't know Don Juan," I said. "What he sets out to do, he does."

That afternoon I took hot food to the officers' quarters and found both men looking rested. Don Juan poured a cup of wine for me.

"Ready to set sail again, Lazaro?" he teased.

"Yes, sir." I was surprised at myself. When I left San Blas, I'd wanted to be free of the sea, the schooner, and the Spaniards. Now I wondered if I wouldn't miss all of them.

"Here comes Ayala," Don Francisco announced. "I thought he'd show up today. Why is he limping?"

Don Juan put that question after the officers had embraced, and Lieutenant Ayala sank down on a cot furnished by the mission fathers.

"Ah, Juan, you had the good fortune," he said, then added with a smile, "or made your own."

He eased his leg into another position. "I've had this almost since we parted. It was a present from Don Diego Manrique. When I took command of the *San Carlos*, I found a loaded pistol in the captain's cabin and picked it up to put away. The bedeviled weapon, as crazy as its owner, fired a double charge into my right foot. I was abed during our entire exploration, and if it hadn't been for Pilot Canizares, we'd never have surveyed San Francisco Bay."

"You shouldn't have been so eager to abandon the *Sonora*." Don Juan laughed.

"Maybe not," Lieutenant Ayala said.

I lingered, for no one told me to go, and I wanted to discover what else had happened to the packet boat.

"The foot wasn't my only worry," Lieutenant Ayala said. "We grounded on the rocks when we left the bay and had to repair our rudder. We ran into winds and seas until I finally limped into Monterey Bay on the nineteenth of September. The frigate had already arrived, and here we've stayed, waiting for you, though truly, *amigo*, I figured you were resting on the bottom of the ocean long ago."

"Never attend a man's funeral until you have proof of his death," our captain said.

"Especially when that man is you. Juan, why did you

go on? And why did you finally turn back? It wasn't for any reason that a cautious subject of the King like myself would consider important."

I waited for Don Juan's answer, remembering the bitterness of his final agreement to turn back.

"You're right. I didn't want to turn back," he admitted. "True, Francisco and I showed up on deck one at a time because we could barely stand. Only Pedro, Lazaro, and Carlos were left of our crew. When Miguel had to go into the hold with the rest of our sick, I knew Fate was against us. No matter what the King decreed, we had to reverse our course."

Lieutenant Ayala wagged his head. "Oh, Juan, Juan, had I been the captain, I would have turned tail long since. It's true enough a man makes his own luck, but there are not many Don Juan Bodega y Quadras in His Majesty's fleet."

He continued in a brisker tone. "As soon as you're ready, we'll set sail, for the mission fathers and the whole settlement are robbing their own tables to feed us—especially you, the heroes. Their supplies are limited, and it would be well to be out of here by early November."

"We'll be ready," Don Juan assured him. "Lazaro, how goes it with the crew?"

"Except for Gil and two others, we're fine."

Back at our own quarters, I found Miguel holding forth to a group from the *Santiago*. To hear him talk, you'd have thought he had navigated the schooner single-handed, but from the smiles on the faces of his listeners, I could see the frigate sailors weren't really fooled.

"You tell a fine sea yarn, Miguel," I taunted when we were alone.

"I'm practicing," he said. "When I get home, I won't have to buy a meal or a drink for months. Lazaro, we have a story that will last a lifetime."

I'd pictured myself telling tales in my village, but somehow that wasn't important now. I changed the subject.

Carlos was already getting his galley in order and assembling food for our journey to San Blas.

We departed on the first of November, but again the sea took over, for a calm left us helpless for three days, still in sight of Monterey. Then a northwester got behind us, and in the next ten days the ships coasted together as far as Cape San Lucas.

Death was not finished with us, for on that day Pilot Perez died and the expedition witnessed his burial. As the water closed over him, I looked at Don Juan. What if death had claimed him? I didn't doubt that all of us would have been lost, too.

On the eighteenth of November we sighted the Tres Marías Islands, and on the twenty-eighth we were back in the estuary at San Blas.

It hadn't changed a bit. I eyed the white rock and smelled the stinking beach. I heard the church bells peal. We had been gone two hundred and fifty days, yet San Blas was just the same. I, Lazaro Sanchez, wasn't, for

I wore pride like an extra poncho. I'd been farther north than anyone in San Blas.

The bells went on ringing, and the port captain dispatched a messenger to Mexico City. The viceroy must be given the news.

"Did you hear what Father Serra in Monterey wrote about the *Sonora?*" Pedro asked me.

"Tell me." Father Serra was chief of the California missions, an important man.

"He called the *Sonora* 'a wonderful little boat' and said that six times its crew was at death's door, but even so her officers took possession of two provinces in the King's name."

I had taken part in those ceremonies. Pedro, who had a gift for gathering news, said that Don Juan and Pilot Mourelle were sending journals, maps, and the ship's log to Mexico City.

"Don Juan sent a letter, too," Pedro concluded. "He's recommended rewards and promotions for every single one of us. You'll be no longer a serving boy, Lazaro, but a mariner."

That wouldn't be much good to me in the village. I understood more and more about the meaning of Don Juan's achievements. He'd added five hundred leagues of territory to Spain; he'd cleared up facts about the formation of the coast; he'd brought assurances that thus far no Russians threatened Spanish territories.

Before our officers went to Mexico City to talk to the viceroy, they called us together. At daybreak, I'd be on my way to the highlands. Miguel would travel in another direction.

Don Juan spoke to each one in turn, praising us.

"It is in my heart that this is only the first expedition," he declared. "If the King sends another fleet into the North, I would not wish to be given a more faithful crew than you who stand before me."

He smiled at us. *"Vaya con Dios,"* he said, and all of us repeated the words after him.

It was more than two years before I stood again on the beach at San Blas, waiting impatiently for the arrival of Don Juan and Don Francisco. Out in the harbor lay our ship, the frigate *Favorita,* our vessel for the voyage. How many things had happened since Don Juan said good-bye to us and went to Mexico City.

He had been to Spain, where wonderful honors had been bestowed upon him. He was raised in rank to a captaincy, and he had been knighted by the King.

He had been placed in command of a new expedition to explore farther on the Northwest Coast and had been in Peru searching for a suitable ship. I remembered that his family hadn't wanted him to go to sea, but to become a lawyer or a professor. They must feel differently now, for what lawyer or professor could have gained the honors Don Juan had?

When I'd been on the *Sonora,* I'd longed for the highlands, but life there now seemed dull. Hoeing corn was monotonous, and when the *patrón* took me into his office to help with accounts, I wasn't much happier.

At last news came that Don Juan was returning to San Blas. I rushed to my father. He sighed and nodded.

"Go with God, my son, for it is clear that your heart is with the sea.

Now I heard a commotion on the other side of the warehouse and saw Don Juan and Don Francisco approaching. The port captain with them talked and gestured, but Don Juan looked toward the water and at the frigate. When he saw me, he stopped short.

"Lazaro!"

In his smile I read approval. Did he see that I was no longer the rebellious cabin boy of the *Sonora?* Did he see that I was taller and broader? Did he sense my eagerness? When he spoke, I was sure that he saw all these things.

"Are you ready to set sail?" he asked.

I drew myself up. I stood at attention, but I could feel my grin stretching from ear to ear.

"Ready, sir," I said. "All I want is to sail with you. For Glory and the King!"

Historical Note

NAMES given by the Spaniards on this expedition have not survived except for Trinidad Bay in northern California. Their Dolores Island on the Washington coast is Deception Island and the cape where Commander Heceta took possession is Point Grenville. Santana's men were killed at the mouth of the Quinault River.

The beautiful Alaskan peak Bodega and Mourelle sighted was Mount Edgecumbe and Cape Deceit was Cape Edgecumbe on the north side of Sitka Sound. The harbor of Remedios, where the Indians guarded their fresh water, was in the center of the west coast of Kruzof Island. The port with the excellent climate, where the Spaniards recuperated, was probably on Suemez Island in the Prince of Wales Archipelago, just inside the entrance to Bucareli Bay. From here they did not stop again until their unfortunate landing at the mouth of Bodega Bay in California. Cape Blanco is a real place on the southern Oregon coast, but the River of Martin Aguilar has never been identified. It may have been Coos Bay or the Umpqua River. Commander Heceta on his way south saw the mouth of the Columbia River, but was unable to examine it because too few men were well enough to handle the longboat.

The knowledge gained on this voyage was so important that the British explorer, Captain James Cook, carried with him a copy of Bodega's diary and sailing instructions when he visited the West Coast of North America in 1778. It was not until Cook's voyage that the cause of scurvy began to be suspected—that it was not an infection but resulted from lack of fresh fruits and vegetables.

Arctic Ocean

ALASKA

Mt. St. Elias

Cape
St. Elias

Mt. Edgecumbe
Cape Deceit

Bucareli Bay

BRITISH COLUMBIA

Fraser R.

Vancouver
I.

WASHINGTON

Juan de Fuca Strait

Dolores I.
(Deception I.)

Quinault R.

Columbia R.

OREGON

Southbound

Cape Blanco

Northbound

Trinidad Head

CALIF.

Bodega Bay

San Francisco Bay

Monterey

Yukon R.

Mackenzie R.

ARCTIC CIRCLE

Pacific Ocean

Route of the SONORA